A Winged Messenger

Sorry awakened at dawn and was up on his elbows, looking out across the lagoon, when a lone Laysan albatross flew by at water's edge. Albatross were seldom seen this far north, but there it was, with its big white body and seven feet of white-and-black wings, their tips as sharp as spears. It glided along without effort and then twisted its head and moaned. He could hear it clearly.

A warning! Jonjen had said that an albatross had come by Bikini a long time ago and moaned. A typhoon hit several days later.

Something terrible was going to happen to their atoll. The *tournefortia* tree had warned about it; now the albatross.

Also by Theodore Taylor

The Cape Hatteras Trilogy

Book 1
Bikini

1

Just before the roosters crowed one day in late March 1944, Sorry Rinamu was awakened by great, angry roars from the sky, louder than rolling thunderclaps. Close as the palm-tree tops. Fast moving.

There'd been no warning that dawn. Thick silence; then the sudden, deep growls from above.

Terrified, he jumped off his sleeping mat, and ran outside the family dwelling, which faced the quiet lagoon. He was wearing homemade shorts of sun-bleached rice-bag material, his usual clothing day or night.

His mother and younger sister scrambled out behind him like frightened geese, almost falling over each other. Teacher Tara Malolo, who was living with them that week, came out, too. His grandfather and grandmother followed. There were high-pitched wails and the screams of *ajiri*, small children, from other village dwellings that faced the beach. Everyone had been deeply asleep, accustomed to the lullaby of the surf, the friendly rustle of the palm trees.

In the shallow gray light Sorry could see eight blue aircraft circling far out over the lagoon, single file, like a flight of pelicans. Then they turned back toward the thatch-walled, thatch-roofed houses, flying so low that Sorry could see the outlines of bobbing heads in the open cockpits. The roars grew again. For a moment, as the planes paralleled the beach, then cut sharply over the north end of the island, he thought they'd unload their bombs. Blow up the houses, kill everyone.

His sister, Lokileni, thought so, too. She stood there in a faded cotton nightshirt, screaming. Slender body shaking. Eyes tightly closed to ward off death.

His *jinen*, his mother, Ruta Rinamu, went to her knees in the sand, praying, eyes closed, the tips of her fingers touching her chin.

Sorry held his breath. His brown eyes were wide with fear. *Please do not kill us!*

His *jimman*, his grandfather, Jonjen, stared at the planes as if his look could drive away the evil vultures. He did not seem afraid.

His *jibun*, his grandmother, Yolo, covered her sunken eyes. She feared ghosts and seldom spoke. She was with the spirits of the wind, the tides, the rains, the fishes. Her skin was like crinkly brown paper stretched over her bones.

Frowning widely, Tara Malolo stared silently at the aircraft.

Others in the village had come out of their houses and were standing or kneeling on the beach in little groups. *Terrified. Frozen. Screaming. Praying.*

The planes continued their second run, coming even lower.

The first one fired a machine-gun burst at the Japanese weather station, north of the houses. The second did the same.

As they flew over again, the palm and pandanus

trees actually quivered. Sorry could feel the heat of engine exhausts and see the flames spitting from them. Explosions always came with the white men.

The free-running pigs squealed and ran in circles. Chickens screeched, frightened silly, too, by the noise. The island's six dogs ran under the small cookhouses to hide.

Sorry covered his ears but kept his eyes open.

Grandfather Jonjen finally identified the dive-bombers and whom they belonged to. He shouted happily, "Amiricaans, Amiricaans! . . ." The planes had white stars on their sides, not the red markings of Japan.

Tara jumped up and down, clapping her hands.

As the throbbing engine noises began to fade, the shout of "Amiricaans" echoed joyously along the beach. There was laughter and hugging, much excitement. Even the bewildered *ajiri* were now smiling, though they didn't know why.

Several of the American navy pilots had waved from their cockpits. One had held up his fingers in a V, the victory sign, new to the islanders.

Americans! White men from the east. Military men.

Perhaps that meant that Bikini, northernmost atoll of the Ralik chain, twenty-two hundred miles southwest of Hawaii, would soon be free of Japanese occupation.

Twenty-six islands and islets, the larger ones palm- and pandanus-tree-covered, formed the atoll, an oval lagoon in the ocean rimmed with coral reefs. Bikini, largest and most beautiful of the twenty-six, was four miles long and less than a half mile wide. All the Rinamus had been born on the island. Only Sorry's late

5

father, Badina Rinamu, and Grandfather Jonjen had ventured beyond the lagoon. Sorry hoped to do that someday, sail to the *ailiñkan*, the outside world.

In five days, he would turn fourteen and officially become a man in island tradition with a family celebration. He was already the main provider of food. He would also become the head of the family, replacing Grandfather Jonjen, who had been acting head since Badina Rinamu died four years ago. Sorry would now be the family *alab*, representing the Rinamus on the village council, with Jonjen as his legal adviser.

There could not have been a better early birthday gift than those roaring planes and waving pilots, that gunfire.

Her fright ebbing away, Lokileni asked, "Will we be free?"

The Japanese soldiers sometimes demanded the bodies of young girls. Lokileni was only eleven, but she was in danger when the soldiers had too much beer or palm wine. So there was good reason for her to fear them, good reason for Sorry to protect her.

"I don't know," he answered, mind whirling. "Let's hope so."

As the engine clatter vanished entirely, the planes becoming dots in the western sky, Sorry looked up the beach toward the gray wooden weather station with its big radio antennae on the roof, target of the machine-gun burst.

The Japanese soldiers were standing outside watching the aircraft disappear. One man had been killed by the second plane. The others were jabbering excitedly. Sorry could hear them faintly.

6

Everyone in the village hated them. They never smiled. They were never polite. The islanders called the squat wooden building *mwen ekamijak*, "house of fear."

Once, about a year ago, the sergeant, their leader, claimed Sorry had insulted him. He'd laughed when he saw the sergeant trip and fall down in the sand. The sergeant had made Sorry bow down a thousand times to the doorstep of the *mwen ekamijak*. A soldier, aiming a rifle at him, had counted.

That night, to prove he was not a coward, Sorry had waited near the barracks, hidden, the family ax in his hand, for the sergeant to come out. But he never did. Finally, Sorry went home to sleep.

From time to time, he'd heard the elders talk of killing the soldiers. Serious talk. And he'd joined in. He was ready to use the ax and help chop them to pieces. But the *iroij*, kindly Chief Juda—descendant of the famed Larkelon, once the highest Ralik chain chieftain—said that many soldiers would then come 250 miles from Kwajalein, a headquarters island, and shoot every man, woman, and child on Bikini. Show no mercy!

Jonjen had said, "Juda is right. If the soldiers don't send a weather message back to their base for two or three days, a seaplane will come to find out why."

"There's nothing we can do?" Sorry had asked, wishing his father were still alive. *He* would fight.

"Nothing," his grandfather answered.

Up to the day in 1942 when the Japanese invaded and mined the lagoon entrance, there'd been peace on the atoll for a hundred years or more. No one had a gun. Sorry had never even seen one until the Japanese

7

arrived. The only land enemies had been flies, scorpions, and palm rats.

Words had been passed along from the outside world, traveling from lonely atoll to lonely atoll like birds on flyways. Outriggers from other atolls and the few ships that ever visited usually entered through Enyu Channel, a wide opening between Enyu Island and Airukji Island. The ships would anchor about a quarter mile off the beach, but the outriggers would ride right up on it. There would be feasts and outsider talk about the wondrous *ailiñkan* for two or three days, then the visitors would go. After they departed, the people would talk about the talking and think about the talking. Sorry had always listened eagerly.

Otherwise, what happened daily on Bikini was sunrise and sunset and the gathering of food from the trees and from the sea and making mats and baskets and walls and roofs and twine and *talk*. Talk about the fish and the weather and each other. The breeze hummed; the pigs rooted; the chickens walked and pecked, walked and pecked. Peace and quiet—until the Japanese arrived.

"Why did they come here?" Sorry had once asked angrily.

"Weather conditions are always important to ships and aircraft," Jonjen had answered.

In the world Sorry knew best, his family lived, worked, laughed, sang, and prayed as if war didn't exist, as if the world stopped at the entrance to the lagoon. Suddenly they were captives, lazy natives, kin to monkeys. The Japanese didn't need to say it. The message was in their eyes: *You are inferior. You are worthless.*

8

"Is it always this way in war?" Sorry had asked.

"I think so. Innocent people everywhere are harmed," Tara Malolo had answered.

Along with everyone else, for the past two years Sorry had watched and listened as the soldiers demanded coconuts, pandanus fruit, preserves, and taro, the starchy tuber plant, in addition to catches of seafood. If twelve reef lobsters were caught, the Japanese demanded six.

Wrinkled Grandfather Jonjen, the village man of God, who walked with a crooked stick and carried the Marshallese Bible almost everywhere he went, said, "The palms whisper 'Peace' all the time, but the soldiers never listen."

Sorry thought that the only good thing the Japanese had done was build catchments—large cisterns of concrete—to trap precious rainwater that flowed down sheets of corrugated iron.

He did not know how long he could contain his anger. He did know that if any soldier raped Lokileni he would use the ax, no matter what might happen to him.

In the 1920s, a new field of scientific research was introduced—study of the nucleus of the atom.

2

Memory of the sight, even the roar, of the planes remained with Sorry through *mabuñ*, breakfast.

In the island tradition, they sat separately: Sorry
and his grandfather; and about eight feet away, his
mother, his grandmother, Lokileni, and Tara. Early
light flooded the serene lagoon.

Behind the single street of crushed pink coral, there
were twenty-six dwellings spread widely along the central part of the island. The eleven families lived out-
doors; their cool, high-peaked pandanus houses, with
movable thatch walls, were mainly for sleeping. In
windy and rainy seasons, the decorated window matting could be unrolled. The song of rain on the leaf roofs
had put Sorry to sleep on many summer nights.

Each clan had its separate small cookhouse, which
was waist high and no wider than a spread of arms, but
everyone was welcome to eat at any fire pit.

Breakfast was always leftovers from the night before. Fish or taro root or coconut meat or octopus or
clams. Sorry and Lokileni always liked *jekaro*, the
sweet sap of broken palm-blossom stalks, for this meal.

"I still don't know why the Japanese and Americans
are fighting," Sorry finally said, sipping the *jekaro*.

11

His mother answered gravely, "I don't know either. But it seems someone is always fighting out there."

Jonjen said solemnly, "It is always land and money, everywhere."

"There has to be more," Sorry said, looking at his grandfather. Though Jonjen's cheeks were sunken like Sorry's grandmother's eyes, his mind was still sharp. Most of his teeth were gone.

Money was not important to the islanders. There was really no place to spend it. The only money they ever received was from copra, the sun-dried meat of the coconut, supplied by twenty thousand-odd trees. First German marks, then Japanese yen. A small steamship would visit twice a year and a merchant aboard would either buy the copra or trade for it. What money they received went to cloth for dresses and trousers, canvas for sails, utensils, or tools. A shopping trip, by canoe, could take many weeks.

If possessions alone were counted, Jibiji Ijjirik was the richest man on Bikini. His family had a hand-powered sewing machine. The Rinamus had traded their six-month village copra share one year for a wooden chest of drawers and the ax.

"Land and money," Jonjen repeated, nodding. "Always land and money, everywhere."

Parcels of land were owned by clan members on each of the larger islands of the atoll. Nothing was more important to a Bikinian than land, even though it was always claimed by the *iroij lablab*, the paramount chief, Jeimata, who did not even live on the atoll. A family without some land, even a small parcel on another island, had not achieved dignity. The Badina Rinamus owned land on Lomlik and Bukor.

In addition to the Rinamus, there were the clans of Ijjirik, Kejibuki, and Makaoliej. They all treated each other as *nuky*, kinsmen.

Still thinking about the Americans, Sorry asked his grandfather, "Will it be the same if the Americans come? Will we be captives again?"

"We are smaller than ants and easy to crush," Jonjen answered. He was that way, seldom answering directly. Seldom a "yes" or "no," often a "perhaps."

Except for the pilots of those planes, Sorry had never seen an American, much less met one. He did not know whether they were cruel or kind. Tara said they were usually kind.

His mother said, "But they may care nothing about the Marshalls. Maybe they'll let all the islands become free if they win. I hope so."

Jonjen said, after swallowing a chunk of charred tuna, "I've told you before, Sorry, that there was a time long, long ago, the time of the whalers—after the Spaniards, and before the Germans—when we were not so peaceful ourselves. Our warriors went out in canoes to raid any vessel anchored here. Any white man who came to the beach was murdered. There was a lot of blood spilled here in the early days." Grandfather Jonjen, like the other old men of Bikini, was a source of island history. Next to Lokwiar, who was eighty, Jonjen was oldest, at seventy-five.

In what beginning was known, he'd said there were seven Ralik clans, all from Namu Atoll. There was fierce fighting between them and the first clans of the Ratak chain. Headbanded warriors in canoes fifty feet long, armed with axes made of giant shells of *tridacna*, the saw-toothed clam, fought. Many were killed.

While Jonjen was talking, the husky, stern sergeant in charge of the weather station, wearing steel-rimmed glasses, walked by them without even glancing up. With him was another soldier carrying a rifle.

That was usual. Everywhere they went, the rifle went, too. It always threatened death, even when not pointed at the villagers.

They were going to Chief Juda's house. Whenever they came up the beach, it was always to give orders to Juda—too mild and giving a man, Sorry thought.

Staring at the soldiers, he asked himself, *What do they want now?* Then he stood up, shaking his head in dismay.

Sorry was barely five feet. His head was crowned with black curly hair. His skin was dark brown. He looked a lot like his late father, who had been short and stocky, a man of quiet strength. All sinew, no fat . . . How Badina died out on the water, no one knew. The mystery troubled Sorry.

The answer to his question about the soldiers came a little later: *No cooking fires and no one on the beach after dark.* Chief Juda could not burn his kerosene lantern, a symbol of his importance.

The Japanese, afraid of invasion, demanded total blackness so the island would vanish in the night.

Tara Malolo said, "We must remain calm."

In September 1933, it occurred to a young Jewish-Hungarian physicist, Leo Szilard, that it might be possible to set up a nuclear chain reaction and construct an atomic bomb.

3

Sorry remembered the first lesson taught by Tara Malolo in the one-room, pandanus-thatched, council place that also served as the school on Bikini Island.

Sitting on a stool cut from a palm trunk, she'd said with a wide smile, "Good morning. My name is Tara Malolo. I am one of yours. I was born on Rongelap. I'm twenty-four years old and with the grace of the good Lord, I'll be here the next few years as your teacher."

She had trained at the missionary college in Majuro, funded by Hawaiians, and she spoke enough English to be able to talk to people from the outside world. She had soft, dark hair and a full mouth, a beautiful smile, and skin the color of oil-rubbed mahogany. She always wore a flower in her long, shining hair, and her cotton dresses from Hawaii had flower prints. Though she was the prettiest woman on the island, the Japanese did not molest her. They respected her as a teacher and were even polite to her; no one else received these courtesies.

She had brought some seeds from Majuro—yellow and red hibiscus, pink bougainvillea and oleander, mango and coral tree. She tended the plants with love, sparingly fed them coconut water during the dry period. They were flourishing, like she was.

The missionary college had provided her with one copy each of books written in Marshallese on geography, history, spelling, and arithmetic; a world atlas; and a blackboard, with chalk. She had debarked from the trading steamer when there was still peace in the mid-Pacific, and did not have a permanent home on Bikini. She stayed with a different family each week so that no one would become jealous.

Along with the thirteen other morning-class students, Sorry sat on a pandanus mat over sand. School for his group was on Monday, Wednesday, and Friday; the young ones attended Tuesday, Thursday, and Saturday. For his class the hours were eight to twelve, with occasional interruptions so they could help net fish in the lagoon. Outside it was sunny and breezy and hot, as usual; a typical winter day.

Adults often craned their heads in through the open spaces that served as windows in the leaf-mat walls to listen to Tara Malolo. In fact, for most of the first year that she taught, regular work by the adults was often neglected. She'd said it was a different school in that no grades were given and no homework assigned, so anyone could participate.

That first morning, in late November 1941, she said, "How many of you know anything about the history of Micronesia and this island in the Marshalls?"

Micronesia was a Greek word for tiny islands. There were more than two thousand of them spread over three million square miles of Pacific Ocean.

Sorry said, "Only what my father and grandfather taught me."

"Well, I don't know what they have taught you, so maybe I'll repeat some of it. And if I tell you something entirely different from what they said, let's talk about it."

Sorry nodded.

He already knew, from Grandfather Jonjen's wisdom, that there were three types of islands in Micronesia: low atolls, barely above sea level, like Bikini; raised atolls, islands pushed up by underwater violence, usually volcanos, some with sand hills two hundred feet high; and high islands with rugged green mountains, like Guam, Palau, and Kosrae.

Bikini's reefs enclosed the blue and jade green lagoon, which was twenty-four miles long, east to west, and fifteen wide, north to south. Because the atoll's islands were so low, Sorry could not see them while standing on the beach. He had to go to the middle of the lagoon in an outrigger canoe to pick up the palm tops on the horizon across the way. Warm water washed the outer edges of the barrier reef on the windward side. Waters within the lagoon were even warmer and comparatively calm, except during summer storms.

Tara held up a large map of the Pacific Ocean and said, "A long, long time ago, thousands of years, many people of Indonesia—here on the map—fled from the Malay warriors of Asia and began to settle Australia and New Guinea. Then, much later, around fifteen hundred B.C., Pacific voyagers probably reached the Marshall Islands, our islands."

"Where are we?" asked Kilon Calep, of the Shem Makaoliej family.

"Way up here, in the Marshall archipelago," Tara replied. "But first let me tell you how we got here, or how some historians think we got here. They believe we became mixed with the dark-skinned people of New Guinea and the Solomon Islands—here. Many of the males of New Guinea have bushy hair. So do our men. So we likely have Indonesian, New Guinean, and Solomon blood in us. Then we, too, settled eastward, island by island, sailing our outrigger canoes. Now, look closely. Micronesia is on about the same latitude as Siam, the Philippines, Central America, and the Sudan in Africa. So it's hot here, and palm trees grow."

Sorry asked, "Do they have palm trees in Africa?"

Tara smiled. "The closest I've been to Africa is Majuro, but, yes, I think they do. Now, again, look at the map. On a north-south line, our islands lie south of Japan and north of New Guinea. Though most of Micronesia is ocean, with an area as large as the United States, there are ninety-five major atolls and large islands, and the total population is somewhere between forty-five and fifty thousand . . ."

"Including us?" Tomaki Kejibuki, of the Uraki Ijjirik family, asked.

"Including us," Tara replied. "Now, how did *you* get here?"

Sorry said, "Grandfather Jonjen said that we came from Wotje, in the Ratak group, around a hundred and fifty years ago."

"I think your grandfather is mostly right, but I question the date. From what I've read, Bikini has been inhabited, more or less, since the seventeen hundreds. Maybe before that."

Sorry asked, "Are we a cowardly people?"

He remembered that his father said they were. They had lost the warrior spirit, he'd said.

Tara laughed, then said, "No, I don't think so. We are a gentle people, living the way we do. I don't think we are cowardly."

"My grandfather said we used to murder the white man."

"He's right about that, too. But we don't anymore, thank goodness."

Sorry fell in love with Tara Malolo that day. Her laughter was musical, and even better, she knew about the *ailiñkan*.

Less than two weeks after that first session in Bikini school, the Japanese attacked Pearl Harbor in Hawaii, and the whole Pacific raged with war.

An Italian physicist, Enrico Fermi, split the uranium atom in 1934, striking the initial sparks of a nuclear chain reaction. It was the first step toward the making of an atomic bomb.

4

Three mornings after the U.S. planes flew over the island, Sorry, who had gotten up to go fishing while it was still dark, broke the silence with a shout: "Ships! Ships!"

Grandfather Jonjen, who never slept much anyway, blew mightily on his treasured pink conch shell, the largest ever found on the atoll. The hollow *Ah-hoooo! Ah-hoooo! Ah-hoooo!* was a warning signal as old as the first warriors.

Again, everyone stumbled out of their dwellings.

A three-quarter moon lit the lagoon, painting it in mellow silver, and Sorry could see the ghostly outlines of two large ships and a smaller one, anchored about two thousand yards from the beach. They had not been there the night before. No lights shone from them. Warships, he guessed.

Soon there was a harsh sound of engines, and coming toward the island were four small, dark shapes separated from each other by several hundred feet. For a moment, he thought they might be Japanese boats. More soldiers to reinforce the men at the weather station. More trouble. More cruelty. More threats.

Jonjen, also straining his eyes to pierce the darkness,

said anxiously, "Oh, I hope they're Americans. I hope. I hope . . ."

His words were spoken as prayer. "Hope" was often said on Bikini. The people *hoped* it would rain; *hoped* the trees would bear much fruit; *hoped* the tuna would school; *hoped* much copra would be made.

As the boats came nearer, Chief Juda shouted, "All women and children to the barrier beach!"

Sorry's mother, grandmother, sister, and Tara started running with the others toward the windward side of the island, across the shallow ravine, where there was thick undergrowth, berries, and edible fruit. But Sorry stood by Jonjen, looking at the white bow curls sprinkled with phosphorus. The boats were moving relentlessly toward the beach, their engines hammering, exhaust rising like silver steam. Sorry suddenly had trouble breathing.

Finally, three landing craft pushed up on the shore, dropping their flat bows. The fourth seemed to have gotten hung up on a coral head about a hundred yards from the beach and was motionless. The engine on that one was roaring, trying to break the boat free. Some of the coral heads in the lagoon were larger than the village dwellings.

Then there were distinct voices. Sorry knew they didn't belong to Japanese soldiers. His fear went away like a school of rabbitfish chased by slashing bonitos. In its place, he felt great relief.

The men who had been in the boats, dim figures bulky with equipment, began to move quickly and almost silently into the palms.

They disappeared into the dark groves, heading toward the weather station. Soon, explosions rang out, and Sorry bolted the opposite way, joining his grandfather and the other fleeing village men. It was not their battle. The Japanese and the Americans had been killing each other for more than two years.

Then the noise stopped and aside from the new voices, it became quiet. The voices were calm, untroubled by what had just happened. No shouting, no harsh words.

Jonjen said, "I think it's safe now."

Though the sun had yet to rise, yellow-gray daylight was spreading quickly, and Sorry returned with the others to the center of the village, near the *monjar*, the church, and the council-school structure. There were several hundred U.S. marines there in full combat gear, talking and smoking. The "battle" of Bikini was already over.

Chief Juda, who had taken time to tug on a shirt and trousers, though his callused feet were bare, said, "Welcome," to the tall marine who seemed to be in charge. Juda could speak two words of English, *welcome* and *good-bye*.

Everyone laughed when the marine replied, "*Yokwe-yuk.*"

In Marshallese, *yokwe-yuk* meant *hello* and *farewell* and *love to you*.

The tall marine, taller by three hands than any Bikinian, wore an olive-colored helmet, and Sorry saw a pistol at his hip. But his eyes were blue and friendly. He smiled, shook hands with Juda, and spoke to his *riukok*, his interpreter, a man from another Marshall atoll, who wore white man's clothing, white man's sunglasses, and a white man's wristwatch.

Addressing the gathered people, the *riukok* said,

"Your troubles are over. Rather than be captured, the Japanese have killed themselves. They were hiding in a bunker."

The plundering and raping were over. The people no longer needed to fear the men in the wooden house. Lokileni and the other women could breathe easier.

The officer spoke again and the interpreter said, "We'll bury the enemy for you and give you all their food supplies and some of their equipment."

"Thank you, thank you," said Juda in Marshallese.

Sorry had heard only what Tara had said about Americans but was immediately impressed with their kindness and generosity. They shared. They were not at all like the Japanese. At least this tall marine wasn't. He again shook hands with Juda when the American flag was raised.

Sorry's mother told Lokileni to run to their house for a seashell necklace, an *alu*.

When Lokileni returned, her mother placed the *alu* around the marine's neck and chanted in Marshallese:

> *This* alu
> *I bring and place upon you*
> *As a reminder of us*
> *On this joyous occasion.*

After hearing the translation the tall marine said solemnly, "I accept on behalf of all my men."

Ruta Rinamu smiled. She had long black hair and a round face and large dark eyes that usually sparkled like the white water of the barrier reef when sun was shining on it. Lokileni had her eyes.

Soon, holes were dug for the enemy soldiers and

they were buried nude near the barrier reef, dumped in without regret or ceremony.

After the burial, Sorry joined the rest of the islanders, who stood lined up while navy doctors checked them for health. There was little sickness on Bikini. The diet of fish, coconuts, and taro was a healthy one.

At sundown, Sorry was on the shadowy beach with everyone else, saying, *"Kommol, kommol"*—*Thank you,* and *All good things to you*—as the Americans returned to their boats.

Then everyone went to the church to thank God for deliverance. Juda lit his lantern, they sang songs, and Jonjen, who always looked distinguished in his white waiter's jacket—a gift of long ago—read Psalm 147 from the Marshallese Bible: "Praise the Lord! For it is good to sing praises to our God . . ."

Then they took dried-palm-frond torches and—singing again, this time "Amazing Grace," Sorry's favorite hymn—went toward the weather station to see what was there. It was a night Sorry would never forget— thirty or forty torches, blazing red, crackling, flowing toward the barracks against the black, calm night, the voices carrying out over the splash of low surf.

The women who had cleaned the wooden building, including his mother and Yolo, already knew what was there—different things from Japan. Tools and food and kimonos and sandals and books and rice bowls and chopsticks and beer. The marines had taken the guns.

Chief Juda said he would divide everything equally among the eleven families when it was daylight.

Sorry saw a thick Japanese magazine with many photographs in it and decided to ask Juda for that gift in the morning.

Several hours later, the American ships sailed off into the night and the islanders began a *kemen*, a celebration.

————

They were richer by eighty big bags of rice and hundreds of tins of fish and red meat and cans of vegetables that no one had ever eaten or even seen before, and life on Bikini would slowly return to normal, Jonjen predicted.

In the morning, Sorry claimed the magazine.

In 1939, world-famous physicist Albert Einstein wrote to U.S. President Franklin D. Roosevelt warning him that Germany had the capability of producing a "horrible military weapon," an atomic bomb.

5

Sorry took his magazine and crossed the ravine to the barrier beach to sit in the shade of some bushes that had thick, waxy leaves. Plants out there had to be tough to withstand the salt spray carried by wind toward the village. He'd often go there alone to think about things and wonder what was beyond the horizon. Sometimes he'd find a mound of bright shells and blossoms, an offering made by Grandmother Yolo to the old gods. It was a lonely place.

Among the trees that grew on the barrier-reef side of the island was the *tournefortia*, its brown, tangled, bare branches looking like long fingers. Grandmother Yolo said it talked at night; she recently heard it say something terrible was going to happen to them. Yolo didn't speak anymore unless the matter was of grave concern.

Sorry was amazed by the pictures in the large magazine. There were buildings ten times as tall as their palm trees. There were ships that seemed to be half as long as the island; there were machines that ran on tracks. Everyone wore clothes. There were many other things that he'd heard about but had never seen. He'd often wondered about that other world, the *ailiṅkan*, and what it was really like. Now, at last, he was seeing it, and he wanted to go there.

He sat under the wax-leaved bushes, near a moist taro pit, for three hours that morning, turning the pages back and forth, the ocean slamming nearby. Then he walked home, thinking that he'd ask Lokileni to make a pocket out of pandanus to store the magazine.

Making mats was woman's work. Men were not allowed to do it. In the old days, women were not allowed to fish from the canoes. From the shore, yes; the canoes, no. There were strict laws. Even now, only men could cook over open fires. Men were not allowed to bake in the *um*, the pear-shaped oven made of piled pieces of coral rock.

Usually, everyone slept at midday, when *al*, the equatorial sun, was hottest. Even the dogs and pigs and chickens slept. The only sound was the flutter of palm fronds, wind being almost constant from December to April. Usually, Sorry slept, too. This day he couldn't. He stayed on his mat and pored over the magazine, looking for two or three minutes at each picture, then looking again. He was hungry for knowledge of the other world.

———

In the afternoon he went about his two main chores, the first of which, gathering green coconuts, he shared with Lokileni. His toes gripped the narrow notches on the palm trunk. As a climber she was as good as he was, but she didn't have the strength to twist off more than two or three.

From the ground, she called up, "Do you see any fish?"

He'd forgotten to look. Everyone who went aloft for coconuts spent a few minutes searching the lagoon for schools of fish that might be moving out there. Frothing water was the sign. The conch would blow. Then canoes would be quickly launched to skim out and drop the nets.

"Can't see any," he yelled back, twisting off a fat coconut.

He remembered the day he'd climbed his first palm, when he was five; how proud his father had been. Water from thirty coconuts was what each family needed daily during the drought season. Rain came only in the summer and the villagers trapped it as best they could, storing it in hollowed tree trunks and large tins, and now in the Japanese cisterns as well.

Without the coconut they could not survive. There was little or no fresh water on the northern low atolls. After the pint of coconut water was drained, the nuts were split and the immature meat was fed to the pigs, dogs, and chickens. Food was never wasted. For centuries they had lived off what the island and the sea gave them.

But it was always the coconut that was the true staff of life. The palm bark, scraped to a powder, would stop open wounds from bleeding. The root, mashed to a pulp, would stop a toothache. In his prayers, Grandfather Jonjen often talked about the amazing coconut.

The only other usable tree was the *bop*, the strange pandanus, which Jonjen said was one of the oldest plants on earth. The female pandanus fruit looked like a pineapple. Jelly from it could be dried and used for food on long ocean voyages. In ancient times even sails were made of pandanus. The hard surface of the long, dry, ribbonlike leaves made perfect roofs and matting. Sorry often chewed the inner end of the pandanus fruit, the orange-colored starchy pulp. The pollen from male flowers, mixed in coconut oil, made a love potion.

And Grandfather Jonjen also remembered the *bop* in his prayers, asking for the tree's good health.

———

As soon as they'd piled the coconuts near the cook-house, Sorry picked out a spear from his father's collection and returned to the barrier reef. He could have walked along the lagoon shore, but the fish there were usually smaller and harder to jab. And he wanted to get back to the magazine. The ocean side provided easier targets, though it was dangerous when the rollers were high—gathering far out, crashing on the lip of the solid reef, sending up salt spray, flooding white foam in, then sucking it out. Some days the sea warned with deafening noise, telling the islanders not to enter it. Other days, it smiled and welcomed visitors.

The sea had been both his friend and his enemy from the time he could just crawl over the sand. Elders always explained to children about the sea, said to watch it and listen to it, hear it speak of love and speak of danger.

Sorry believed his father had died somewhere along the barrier reef. Badina had not been in a canoe that day, fishing in the lagoon. He'd taken a spear and headed for the reef. That much was known. Sorry believed a shark had gotten him, probably a vicious tiger, while it swam in the inshore waters looking for a finned target. His body was never found. Sorry was always very careful when he speared in the reef waters.

This day the waves were moderate, and he went beneath where they were breaking, swam under them, and came up in clear water, with blue coral heads and waving sea grass beneath him. Rainbows of fish were down there, going in and out of the coral valleys, caverns, and passages. There were wrasse and grouper and blacktail snappers and the usual smaller schools of pink and yellow and green. He saw a moray eel ducking into a crevice, there to await a meal.

He was wearing a pair of homemade goggles, eyepieces he'd carved from hardwood with glass lenses from a washed-up bottle, broken and shaped by rubbing on coral. Diving, he could keep his eyes open. The goggles were attached to his head by *sennit*, palm twine. It was made by rolling coconut fiber between the hand and thigh, forming a thread an eighth of an inch thick. *Sennit* was strong enough to hold a sixty-pound tuna. By old law, women could not roll *sennit*. He'd rolled yards of it.

He floated, barely pumping his feet, waiting for a chance to shove the sharp spear into a log grouper. Finally, one nosed within range, and he got it just behind the head. The wrist noose from the spear tightened as the grouper thrashed and pulled him deeper. He'd speared there before, and now he planted his feet on a smooth ledge of coral, jerking his head out of water to breathe. The grouper tugged and thrashed but finally gave up, and Sorry towed it back to shore.

He could not remember a time when he didn't swim. The lagoon and barrier-reef waters were second homes.

Out again in the surf, toward the drop-off, he spotted a bigger one, a grouper of ten or eleven pounds that would give the family two days of meals. It was coming up out of the murk, paying no attention to the shadow of Sorry's body above. It swam on up to a party of butterfly fish and gobies, set on having a meal.

The spear punched a hole in its side to the rear of the gills, spilling blood out in a red cloud. Sorry heaved back. Then out of the corner of his eye he saw a great blue-gray shape coming fast.

Mako, he knew, fastest shark in the Pacific.

A shark that might or might not attack. The lemon and the nurse and the blackfin and the whitetip and the sand shark were seldom problems. The hammerhead, the gray reef shark, and most dangerous of all, the tiger, drove divers out of the water, hearts pounding. But no one could ever tell what was on the tricky mako's mind.

Today it rolled its pointed head to take the grouper and spear in one bite.

Rather than be pulled down into the darkness where the mako lived, Sorry slipped the wrist noose off and swam back to the surface, soon returning home with the first fish. He could easily make up for the loss tomorrow at the same spot, shark or no.

The living reef and all the life around it would be there tomorrow, as it had been for more years than man could count, Sorry knew. Tiny animals made the coral from seawater lime, then died, leaving their empty dwellings to be filled with hidden food. Turn a stone, and snapping shrimp could be heard. Lift seaweed and find a spider crab. Small octopus lived all over the reefs. They writhed and wrapped tentacles around Sorry's head and throat until he killed them with a bite.

At sunset, often the most beautiful time of day, Sorry was again looking at the magazine. He couldn't get enough of it.

Grandfather Jonjen, sitting nearby in the sand, watching him, asked, "What do you see in there, Sorry?"

"I see things I didn't know existed. Look at this building. See how tall it is." He showed Jonjen the building. "Did you know about places like this?"

"I've heard . . ."

"And would you like to go inside them and look around?"

Jonjen shook his head. "I don't think so."

He was hopeless, Sorry thought. Grown very old on this small island, seldom having left the atoll lately, all he could do was read his Bible every day and find something in it to talk about on Sunday.

Sorry turned the page and pointed to a train. "This," he said. "Would you like to ride on it?"

"I don't think so," said Jonjen, yawning.

He *was* hopeless. He still had his tools from the old days—shark's-tooth awls and shell knives. He had four-inch trolling hooks made of pearl shell. They were fifty years old. The young men were gathering modern steel tools and fishing tackle from the outside world, but not Jonjen.

Jonjen could walk out into a grove and weave a green basket or hat from the fronds within minutes: the old ways. Sorry could do that, too, but he didn't plan to practice the old ways.

He loved his *jimman* but didn't want to be like him.

Two days later, just before the atoll council was to meet for the first time since the Japanese occupation ended, his *jimman* demanded that they talk. Sorry said he had bad feelings about becoming an *alab* and sitting with the council, men twice or three times his age. They would laugh at him, scorn him, he believed.

Jonjen said, "You must."

"Unless you are sick or insane," his mother added. "You are neither, Sorry."

"I'll sit beside you in the beginning," Jonjen promised.

During the occupation, the council had met only twice, both times over property disputes on the outer islands. It met only when a decision was needed.

"I won't know what to say," Sorry insisted.

"You'll learn," Jonjen said. "It is usually simple. You think about it, whatever it is, then vote what you think."

"It's your time, Sorry," his mother said firmly. "When you become fourteen, you must use your mind as well as your muscles."

"Yes, Sorry, you must do that," Tara said.

They were out by the cookhouse. Sorry's mother was making *lukop*, a pudding, from *jekaro*. The sap had many uses. Now and then she mixed it with grated coconut to make a candy, *amedama*. It could also be boiled into syrup to pour over taro.

Sorry stuck his finger in the wooden bowl and raked out a daub of the sweet stuff. "But, Grandfather, if you are there to tell me how to vote, I'm not needed . . ."

"I'll go with you five or six times."

Sorry licked his fingers, blew out a breath, and shook his head.

His mother said, "Your father would be so proud to see you there."

Sorry sighed. Why couldn't they understand how foolish and ignorant he'd feel sitting there with the older men, afraid to open his mouth if he did have an opinion? And the idea that he'd suddenly become another person simply because he'd turned fourteen was wrong. He hadn't changed overnight.

He looked at his mother, at Tara, and then at his *jimman*. "I'll do it jointly, and only if we tell everyone that we are both *alab*s but will vote as one."

There. That would make the ghost of his father, somewhere along the barrier reef, proud and happy.

Grandfather Jonjen allowed a narrow smile.

On January 19, 1941, President Roosevelt approved research toward the making of an atom bomb.

6

Nantil was an island five miles to the northwest, between Bikini and Aoeman. It was about one mile long and a quarter mile wide. Sorry had gone there with other boys five or six times, sometimes staying overnight, mainly to get away from home.

Today he was going alone to celebrate his coming of age and his assuming responsibility for the family. It was an island tradition.

Many atoll males had done this over the years, going away to one or another atoll island for a night or two simply to be alone for a while, not see the same faces as every day, not hear the same voices. They'd gone to places where they could think about a lot of things. His father had done it off and on. Once, after an argument with Sorry's mother, Badina went to Bokabata, up in the northwest corner, and stayed for a week.

You could walk very slowly from one end of Bikini to the other in less than an hour. There wasn't a single secret that could be kept overnight in all that closeness, and it was a wonder there wasn't a fistfight every so often in or between families. Yet Sorry couldn't recall any. Maybe it was the soft air and the quiet in the necklace of white-and-green islands that kept an even-tempered peace. But sometimes the closeness was overwhelming.

Nantil had never been permanently inhabited by humans, so far as was known. It had a nice grove of palms and about sixty scattered pandanus. Sorry liked its barrier reef's crevices and holes, dwellings for the clawless lobsters. He'd dug in the sand for turtle eggs. The usual fish population was there as well.

The moon would be full this night for the second time since the Japanese killed themselves, and in midmorning he loaded some bed matting into one of the small canoes along with a piece of fish netting, two spears, and the magazine. Lokileni had made the pandanus pouch he'd asked for to protect it against the weather. The magazine was his prize possession. He slid the canoe into the water, pulled up the sail, and headed for Nantil. The wind was steady and moderate; the canoe skated through wavelets. It was usually a paddling craft, so he'd rigged the sail himself.

Marshall Islands double-enders, with their high, narrow hulls and arched outriggers, were known throughout the South Seas for speed and handling, riding out sudden storms, and spilling wind from the cloth sail. The island had eight big canoes, capable of high-seas sailing, twenty-five or thirty feet in length, with twenty-foot masts. It took two or three men to sail one. Then there were three smaller canoes, for in-shore lagoon travel, that Sorry could handle alone.

His father had taught him how to fish and sail; his *jimman* had taught him the stars and how to navigate the way Polynesians and Micronesians had done centuries ago. They used stick charts, *mattang*, made from palm-frond ribs bound together with *sennit*, and plotted the islands, working with a knowledge of wave patterns, of how they slapped against the bow of a canoe.

Jonjen had told him the stories he'd heard as a boy. The old religion was tied to the stars, planets, the sea, the sun. When a long voyage was scheduled, hundreds of miles, the warriors prayed to their god, Ani, for fair winds and safety. They would wait for days, until their priest gave them Ani's blessing.

Sometimes Sorry imagined himself back in those days, sailing with nine other strong men in canoes fifty feet long, five or six canoes abreast, singing war songs, going far, far away; not returning for months. Skimming along now, he was thinking of those men in their great canoes, bound for other lands. How long would it be before he could go, too?

He reached Nantil in less than an hour. Going home, against the wind, would take longer. Without humans around, birds owned the island. Reef herons, terns, tattlers, black and brown noddies, red-tailed tropic birds, and gulls rose from the sands, squawking as he pulled the canoe up above the tideline. There were hundreds of nests in the sand and brush.

He shouted a *yokwe* at them, knowing that if he got too near any of their nests they'd attack. From other trips to Nantil and some sharp pecks on the head, he'd learned to avoid the nests if possible. Once, the birds had bloodied him.

The *hak*s, the black frigates, with seven-foot wingspans, were dangerous at nesting time. They were out feeding when he arrived, soaring over the sea with their wings held motionless, waiting for other birds to dive on fish, then robbing the catch. They didn't have web feet and didn't land on water.

He had in mind combing the beach and looking for shells, looking at the magazine again, picking coconuts to take back, and then going after lobster on the barrier reef when night fell and the moon was overhead. He was alone and celebrating his manhood and could do whatever he wanted.

There'd been a tragedy on Nantil the past year. An Ijjirik boy—August, a year younger than Sorry—had come over to spend the day, along with an older cousin, Jasua. It was Jasua who told everyone what had happened.

Arriving, they saw a big, round metal object washed up on the sands. It had horns.

Jasua told August not to touch it. He thought it had something to do with the war. August didn't listen, and after Jasua walked off, he pounded on one of the triggering horns with a giant clamshell. Jasua said the explosion knocked him down where he was, several hundred yards away. There wasn't even a piece of August to bury. He had tampered with one of the Japanese mines that had slipped its mooring on the bottom of the lagoon.

Poor August. Poor Nantil. The boom was heard on Bikini.

Until today Sorry hadn't been back to Nantil, and he had told no one except family he was going. He didn't think anyone else had visited recently, either. The people of the Marshalls, especially the older ones, like Yolo, believed in evil spirits. They saw the death as being caused by an evil spirit, as if August had heard a *yilak* say, "Pound on the horn."

Since no one had come near Nantil in almost a year, there were many coconuts on the ground, sprouting palm blossoms, as well as many green ones in the trees. The past season's pandanus clusters had fallen and were rotting in the sand.

There were harsh bird cries, the usual palm flutters, and the rumble of the ocean at the barrier reef. No shouts from Bikini children at play, no sounds of a canoemaker hollowing a log, no murmur of the women as they plaited pandanus. He'd left all that behind to be alone.

He plunged into the lagoon and rolled like a porpoise, swam out a bit, then turned back toward shore. In the waist-high water he could see the garden below. Oarweed and waving, green sea fan, bright blue moss and red sea cucumbers, scarlet and yellow sponges, fish in every color.

Then he walked along the lagoon beach and found things washed ashore from the American ships that had freed the islands: empty boxes, empty bottles, a wooden chair, and many other objects he could not identify. Similar things had washed up on Bikini beach after the ships departed. He made a pile near the canoe to take home and share. The chair would go to his family, joining their chest of drawers. He spent almost two hours walking the shore and adding to the pile.

After that he looked for shells. There were a lot more now than on his past trip to Nantil. There were moon shells and tiger cowries and cat's eyes and helmets, and he gathered them in a canvas navy bag that had floated to the beach. Those would be for Lokileni. He found three empty conch shells to give away. Scavengers, conch lived on the sandy bottom and moved slowly, in jerks. Tiny crabs had made homes in the empty shells.

As he walked he thought about the last conversation he'd had with Tara. They often talked. She'd said to wait until he was eighteen to leave the island, then find a way to Kwajalein or Majuro, get a job of any kind, and eventually go on to Hawaii, finish schooling, and enter college. That would be his goal, he decided. Four more years. Tara hoped the war would be over by then. But who would head the family? That bothered him.

When the sun was highest, he climbed for green coconuts, drank their water, ate some pandanus fruit, and got into the shade to look, once again, at the magazine. By now, he'd probably looked at it a hundred times. Pages were ragged around the edges.

Each time, he'd found something new to study and think about. There was the laughing Japanese boy on a sled in that expanse of white he'd learned was called *snow*; there was another boy riding a two-wheeled machine on a country road. Tara had told him about machines.

Then he came to war pictures. Soldiers marching and aircraft flying and ships spouting black smoke and shooting big guns. He could not understand how the same people who were having fun in the snow and riding the machine were also fighting a war.

Confused about the habits of the people of *ailiñkan*, he finally fell asleep, thinking of August and what had happened several hundred feet away. There was still a crater in the sand where the mine had exploded at the high-tide line. The sand there was black.

In June 1942, the Manhattan District, a U.S. scientific-military organization, was established to continue nuclear fission research, which might lead toward the making of an atom bomb.

7

Sorry awakened when the sun was a quarter of the way to the horizon, ran down to the lagoon, and plunged in, then got a spear from the canoe and began walking toward the barrier reef. As he neared the ocean, moving by the windward brush, threading through the last palms on that side, he was suddenly face-to-face with an angry *hak*, its wings stretched to the full seven feet. Guarding a nest of chicks, the frigate let out a throat rattle and Sorry backed down to the edge of the water, aiming his spear at the bird.

Within a few minutes he had a blacktail snapper flapping on the tip of the spear. He killed it with the usual bite behind its head, then circled back to where he was camping. He scaled the fish with a shell and ate some of it uncooked.

As twilight, with all its shades of Pacific blue, began to cast shadows in the palm grove, the bird cries grew fewer and softer, except for an occasional outburst. Sorry took up the magazine and started at the front again. He wondered again why the Japanese people, with all their wonderful machinery, couldn't live in peace.

When darkness finally spread over the lagoon and island, he put the magazine away in the plaited pouch and waited for the moon to rise. When full, or near full, the moon gave the night hunter the gift of light, shining down on the shallow, low-tide water on the shelf inside the barrier reef. The tide would be high again in a few hours, higher than at any other time during the month.

If the ocean was behaving, the hunter could always see the glistening blue-green backs of clawless lobsters that lived down in the outer reef's crevices and canyons and came up on the knee-deep, clear-water inner shelf at night to feed. It was easy to spear them in the ivory light. So at the time of full and near-full moon, there were feasts in the village.

When the moon had risen a quarter of the way up from the sea, a white-orange ball in the eastern sky, it took Sorry no more than an hour to get a lobster each for the eleven families. He put them in the netting he'd brought along, pulled it tight with twine, and then staked the net in a tide pool for pickup in the morning. He knew the same thing was happening over on Bikini. A dozen men would be out with their spears.

Later, when the moon was overhead and beginning its descent to the west, he bedded down. The day had been a good one. Tomorrow morning he'd pick green coconuts and then set sail for home.

Best of all, he'd been alone, thinking no thoughts except the ones he wanted to think. He'd done everything exactly as he'd planned. That was what his father had done on Bokabata, and he had come home happy.

Yet, all day here on Nantil, he knew he hadn't really been alone. August was still around, just as everyone who had died and was buried on Bikini was still there, according to Grandfather Jonjen. Grandmother Yolo believed they walked the beach at night.

Before the time that Yolo had entered her world of near silence, she'd told Lokileni and Sorry stories of Micronesian demons and ghosts and demigods and trees and fish that spoke. Mwoakilloa was home to the lazy giant Lodup. Ebadon, an islet of Kwajalein, was home to a female demon who kidnapped the four children of Likidudu. Yap lagoon was the home of a *galuf*, a monstrous sea lizard. Lokakalle, a murderer, lived on Ijoen, an islet of Arno Atoll. As a child, Sorry couldn't get enough of old Yolo's stories.

Bedded down so close to where August had been torn to little pieces, Sorry felt his presence and remembered him, but not in a frightened way. In his mind, August was saying that the war had killed him on Nantil and he'd done nothing to cause it. The selfish war itself had done it.

Sorry remembered August's smiles, his laughter. They'd fished together, played games together, wrestled in the surf and sand, raced along the beach, come to this very island together. He remembered August's solemn face, his warm eyes.

Suddenly, he was looking at the moon through tears. He knew he could never return to Nantil. It was too painful. He wept about August and suddenly found himself weeping about his father. He cried until his ribs hurt and then finally fell asleep.

———

He awakened at dawn and was up on his elbows, looking out across the lagoon, when a lone Laysan albatross flew by at water's edge. Albatross were seldom seen this far north, but there it was, with its big white body and seven feet of white-and-black wings, their tips as sharp as spears. It glided along without effort and then twisted its head and moaned. He could hear it clearly.

A warning! Jonjen had said that an albatross had come by Bikini a long time ago and moaned. A typhoon hit several days later.

Something terrible was going to happen to their atoll. The *tournefortia* tree had warned about it; now the albatross.

In December 1942, Enrico Fermi and his team of physicists set atomic elements into a self-sustaining nuclear chain reaction on a snow-covered squash court of the University of Chicago. Known as Chicago Pile Number One, it was the second major step toward the making of an atomic bomb.

8

"It moaned just as it passed by me," Sorry said, the sight and sound of the big white-bodied bird lingering on in his mind.

"Albatross often do that," his grandfather said. "But they don't come near here very often."

They were by the canoe shed. Sorry was unloading all the things he'd picked up on Nantil. Lokileni, Tara, and Sorry's mother were a few feet away, watching.

"Maybe it was lost," Sorry said.

"They come around occasionally," his mother said. "Years ago, one followed your father's big canoe for three days. He was going to Wotje. They ride the ocean air currents and follow ships or boats. Why, I don't know."

Jonjen, sitting cross-legged in the sand, said, "They are not a good omen."

Sorry's mother looked over at her father. "I thought you'd say that."

"Remember the typhoon," Jonjen said darkly, his eyes fixed on her with annoyance.

"Of course I do," she answered. The lagoon waters had swept over the island waist deep, destroying all the dwellings and flooding the taro pits. Everyone took to the swayback palms, holding on to *sennit* loops. "No albatross caused it."

"The albatross was carrying a message from God, a warning. We'd sinned," Jonjen insisted.

Sorry's mother gave up. Arguing with her father was useless.

Sorry said, "Let's hope we don't have another one."

He had been seven when that storm hit, and he'd had nightmares for months.

Typhoon season, especially in the western Pacific, was between July and October. Bikini wasn't on the usual typhoon route. But he couldn't think of anything else the albatross might be warning them about.

Other families had come to the canoe shed to look at what he'd found on Nantil. Most of the time beach-combing was best on the barrier reefs, though the waves sometimes smashed things against the coral shelves. Things that floated ashore in the lagoon were usually from ships anchored there.

Chief Juda would soon divide up what Sorry had found on Nantil, except the fine wooden chair. Sorry would keep it for his family. He couldn't guess why the white men had thrown it overboard.

––––––––

The rainy season arrived a month later, and just in time. The islanders had used a lot of coconut water since the past October. The tropical rainstorms of the summer months were often downpours, the heavy, dark clouds draining water over the atoll, curtain after curtain of it.

But the first rain was gentle, and they ran around capturing, as always, what they could in anything that would hold water. Sorry went to sleep that night hearing the pleasant drum of raindrops on the thatch roof.

The first real storm that year arrived during the day a few weeks later, adding more precious water. With it came thunder and lightning, unusual for the north Marshalls. This time there were wind gusts that shook the dwellings and drove the rain inside; the cisterns overflowed.

Sorry could tell when a big summer storm was approaching. The air became hotter and stiller. Ripples began to appear in the lagoon, though he couldn't feel a breeze. The sun disappeared behind haze before the sky turned blue and black. Then the surf would begin to sing in a deeper voice.

The rainy season usually ended with a last storm in early November. Until it arrived again the next summer, Bikini might have a few light squalls, the rain shimmering through sunshine, barely dampening the sand. The sun would quickly dry the island.

No typhoon came roaring out of the west that year. Perhaps the albatross and the *tournefortia* tree had been wrong.

In 1943, on a long mesa extending from the Jemez Mountains, near Santa Fe, New Mexico, work began on the production of an atom bomb. The Los Alamos laboratory was instantly the most highly guarded, secretive place in America.

9

Two months after the albatross, Sorry's uncle, his *ri-korān*, Abram Makaoliej, his mother's brother, sailed into the lagoon unexpectedly. By himself, he'd steered an eighteen-foot outrigger canoe from Eniwetok, about 170 miles away—a voyage full of risk. He'd been away a long time. Sorry's mother had thought her brother was dead.

Abram had brought his personal possessions in a canvas bag, as well as white people's games and other gifts for the family. He'd also brought a guitar wrapped in a yellow raincoat.

"Aha! You thought I was dead!" he shouted, standing in the wet sand of the lagoon shore like an actor onstage. "But I do not die so easy!"

His grin was as bright as the sun; his square face was carefree. His hair was South Seas curly, black as sea urchins.

Sorry was openmouthed.

Abram had "jumped" an American merchant ship in Eniwetok harbor, left it without permission, and then "borrowed" the canoe. He could be put in jail for leaving the ship, as well as for stealing the outrigger. He seemed not to give either act a thought.

Sorry's mother had talked about him many times. "A wild man," she said. "Fearless!"

"A crazy man," Jonjen had said, with a laugh and a shake of head. "He once wrestled a big octopus, underwater, at Lomlik. I saw him do it. He was not much older than you, Sorry."

And here he was, of medium island height and weight, heavily muscled. He had intense eyes, darker brown than his skin, and that wide, shining *al* grin. He was thirty-two years old.

"Where is Badina?" he asked.

Mother Rinamu blinked and swallowed. "He's dead. Four years ago. He disappeared along the barrier reef. He was spearing."

Abram took her into his arms and held her a moment. "He was a good man."

She nodded.

"And who is this?" he then asked, looking at Sorry standing in awe by the prow of the stolen outrigger, water lapping at his toes.

"Our *manje*, Sorry." The firstborn.

Abram extended his hand in a hard grip. To Sorry it was like touching lightning. "We will have fun, *manje*, you and I," Abram promised.

Lokileni, as well as almost every villager who was not out fishing, was also there, having been summoned by Jonjen and the *Ah-hoooo!* of his conch. A son of the island had returned, alive and well.

"And you are the sister," he said to her. "So pretty you are."

Thin-legged, dark-haired Lokileni, in her oversized faded Mother Hubbard dress, lowered her head and smiled at the sand.

Sorry saw Tara watching the stranger with interest. In turn, Abram's eyes lingered on her.

Then he took a look around. "A few more houses, a few more palms, a few more pandanus. It hasn't changed, this island, has it? But what's that wooden one?" He nodded north, up the beach.

"That's where the Japanese lived," Sorry said.

Abram frowned widely. "They were here?"

"Yes," Chief Juda admitted.

"And you didn't kill them?" Abram was frowning at everybody in disbelief.

"We thought about it," Jonjen said. "We talked about it . . ."

"How many?"

"Seven."

Abram snorted. "Only seven? I'm sorry I wasn't around."

Having known him less than five minutes, Sorry thought his uncle would have taken care of the Japanese overnight. Cut their throats one by one. He was not a coward.

Sorry's mother broke in. "I'm glad you weren't here, Abram. None of us would be alive." She had said Abram was ferocious, like the ancient warriors of the northern Marshalls.

Abram laughed and hugged her. "I need some cloth."

"For what?" she asked, beaming at him.

He was clad in a blue shirt, khaki trousers, and brown leather shoes. White man's clothing. "For the old thing."

Jonjen said, "The old thing is over, except for work."

The "old thing" was a loincloth.

Foreigner clothing was now prized. Some of the men

were wearing Japanese army shirts, hats, and pants, courtesy of the deceased occupants of the wooden house. Some were wearing Japanese shoes. All the girls and women wore the tentlike Mother Hubbard dresses. Sorry knew they dated back to the first missionaries, who came in 1904, when the Germans still ruled the Marshalls. Only when fishing in boats or netting or spearing along the shore did the men wear loincloths now. Sorry did, too, for work, sometimes.

But Abram insisted on a loincloth. He said he'd been wearing foreigner clothes all the time he was away. He laughed. "My privates should be comfortable, day and night."

Then he scanned the tops of the nearby palms, eyes alight, and said, "There is not a single coconut left on Eniwetok. The bombs and shells blew them off. I haven't climbed a tree or had a drink of the water in years."

Sorry watched as Abram dropped his trousers and sprinted to a swayback palm—the easiest to climb—and went up, shouting over his shoulder, "My feet have grown soft!"

Twisting a nut off, he dropped it to the sand, then backed down, making fun of his soft soles. "The first thing I have to do is make them tough again," he shouted. Soft feet always had trouble with palm bark and coral.

All over the groves, sharpened hardwood sticks stood upright in the sand. A coconut was peeled by shoving its husk down on the stick, then twisting to pry off the outer shell. Abram did this, then punched an eye out of the nut and drank deeply. The juice ran down his chin and throat.

There was a feast that night, to celebrate the safe homecoming of Abram Makaoliej. He was clad in his new loincloth. The women giggled when he swooped in front of them playfully, flirting with them, laughing. Tara Malolo watched him with amusement. He played white men's songs on his guitar. He could speak English.

Sorry couldn't take his eyes off the stranger. He'd actually been to *ailiñkan*, he'd been there! There was a large, ragged scar on Abram's right side, starting above the ribs and going down to his stomach. In time, Sorry would ask him how he got it.

Everyone ate and sang and danced most of the torch-lit night. Feet stomped steadily on coral sand to the clicking of hardwood sticks and Abram's slap of cupped hands on his bare chest and thighs. His grin was like a torch, Sorry thought. Following tradition, the men danced with men, the women with women.

Abram Makaoliej was home at last.

At Trinity Flats, New Mexico, a place Spanish conquistadores had called *Jornada del Muerto*, the Journey of Death, the first full-scale test of an atomic bomb was conducted at 5:30 A.M., July 16, 1945. Witnesses were speechless at the force and size of the explosion. Acres of the alkali sands were melted into glass.

10

Abram slept late on his mat, weary from his long voyage and the celebrating. When he awakened and ran down to the beach, diving into the lagoon, Sorry followed him to the water's edge.

Naked as an eel, laughing, Abram kicked and bobbed up and down, shaking sparkling droplets from his head. He'd forgotten that only girls and women could bathe in the lagoon; men had to bathe on the ocean side, in barrier-reef pools. The missionaries had seen to that. Sorry was hesitant to remind him. Perhaps someone else would.

When Abram finally stood up in the shallow water, he made a joke. "The water feels the same."

How did it feel fifteen years ago? Sorry was almost afraid to talk to Abram, show his ignorance. He had nothing to talk about. Compared to Abram and Tara, Sorry believed, he knew absolutely nothing.

Abram nodded up toward the village. "Same, same," he said.

In the midmorning shade of the palms, the women were going about their usual work of preparing food, weaving mats, sweeping around the dwellings. They took care of the coral pebble paths and street. Some of the men were out on the lagoon trolling for yellowfin tuna or wahoo: meals for tomorrow. Sorry would join them in the afternoon.

Other men were repairing nets or working on the outriggers in the canoe shed. The islanders were seldom idle, except at midday and on Sundays.

"Same, same," Abram said again, nodding. "I think we hunt for a shark tomorrow."

Sorry couldn't believe what he'd just heard. Home less than two days, Abram wasn't satisfied with lagoon fishing.

"All right," Sorry said, already excited. "I know where a big mako lives."

"The one I have in mind is bigger," Abram said. "Meanwhile, I want to walk around the island by myself. I have many memories."

Sorry nodded, and off went Abram and his memories.

He watched as his uncle stopped by the nearest fire pit, one belonging to the Ijjirik clan, and dug around in the hot coral stones with a stick. Abram pulled up baked taro.

Then he walked slowly north, eating, deep in thought. He was a little bowlegged, Sorry saw. The muscles bulged in his legs and buttocks, visible on either side of the loincloth. His uncle Abram must have worked very hard on those merchant ships.

Yes, Abram could easily have killed all of those Japanese soldiers, easily strangled them, Sorry thought.

———

Back at the family dwelling, two hundred-odd feet up the beach slope and across the street, Sorry said, "We're going shark fishing in the morning."

"Who is 'we'?" his mother asked.

She was plaiting a mat with a needle, the long wing bone of a tattler—all needles were made from bird bones. The young pandanus leaves were dried near the cooking fire, then plaited. He'd seen her plaiting hundreds of times, usually sitting with other women in one or another of the houses. Sometimes they sang hymns. Tara and his near-silent grandmother were there now, plaiting, too.

"Uncle Abram and myself."

"Let him go alone," his mother advised.

Yolo nodded her head. Tara studied Sorry's mother. Alarmed, Sorry protested. "No, no . . ."

"Did he tell you why he's going shark fishing so soon?"

Sorry shook his head.

Mother Rinamu stopped making the mat. "About fifteen years ago Abram was fishing off the Rojkora barrier reef and speared a tiger shark. Somehow, Abram got the harpoon line around his ankle and was dragged overboard. The shark took him toward the bottom. If he'd lost his knife he wouldn't be here today. He cut the line, and then the shark came back on him, jaws open. That scar that he has on his right side was put there by the tiger. Abram almost died. He said he'd get that shark someday."

"He's been waiting all this time?"

"I think so. That's Abram."

"And he thinks the tiger is still there?" Perhaps fate had brought Uncle Abram home? Perhaps he could avenge the death of Badina Rinamu?

His mother shrugged and laughed. "Maybe it is. Abram will find out."

"I will go with him," Sorry said.

His mother nodded. "I guess you'll be safe with any man who can sail here from Eniwetok by himself."

Tara smiled, nodding, too. "Probably," she said.

Sorry had gone fishing thousands of times. Hand line, trolling, spearing, netting—starting when he could barely walk. But nobody fished for the tiger. They attacked canoes. Yet Uncle Abram wasn't afraid.

———

This week, Tara was again staying with the Rinamu family.

Sorry said, "I saw you looking at my uncle last night."

"I think everyone looked at him."

"But you looked at him in a special way . . ."

She just laughed and shook her head.

"You did!"

"He's a handsome man and has a wonderful smile."

Her own smile said as much as her words.

In July 1945, the cruiser USS *Indianapolis* sailed from San Francisco, carrying elements of an atomic bomb named Little Boy. She delivered her top-secret cargo to the island of Tinian, in the Marianas group, a long-range bomber base.

11

Sorry and Abram pulled the Eniwetok outrigger from the canoe shed and slid it down to the water, setting sail to go south past Bokantuak and Eomalan, then around Rojkora, leaving the lagoon to head along the barrier reef and look for the tiger over the steep underwater cliff that dropped almost straight into dark ocean depths.

The wind was light but steady a few minutes past sunrise, and the double-end canoe, under the lateen sail, cut a path through the water. Abram sharpened the steel harpoon head with a stone as they glided along. The *zisst, zisst, zisst* made a pleasing sound, adding to the song of the water and the low hum of the wind on the sail.

"Mother told me about the tiger shark."

Abram lifted his eyes from the gleaming tip of Sorry's father's favorite harpoon. "Someone might have sent him to fish heaven by now. But I doubt it. Not that one. Tigers are as bad as the great white shark of colder water. Both are killers."

Sorry nodded. Jonjen had seen a tiger slice a man in half off Lokwor. "How big was he when he bit you?"

"Seven feet, perhaps. A young one," Abram said

thoughtfully. Then he added, with a laugh, "He wouldn't let me measure him."

"If he's alive, how big is he now?"

"Eleven or twelve feet, I'd guess. Maybe more."

Sorry had seen them seven or eight feet long. The young ones had dark stripes, but as they became older the stripes faded to a mottled gray. Their bellies were stark white. Their noses were not as sharp as the makos', and their mouths stretched from one side of their blunt heads to the other. They had spike teeth. Just the sight of them sent a hot stab of fear into swimmers or men in outriggers.

"Do they stay near home?"

"I think they do," Abram said. "Why?"

"I've always believed a tiger killed my father. There was no trace of him along the reef."

"That's the mark of a tiger, all right."

Sorry was thoughtful for a moment. "And if you spear the same one again?"

Abram chuckled. "I won't let the line get around my feet, you may be sure. I won't make that mistake twice. And I want you to stay in the stern, feet up, if I do hit him."

The line was coiled at the bow. It was strong, new line taken from the Japanese barracks.

"I hope we find him," Sorry said.

Abram nodded and ran a thumb over the harpoon head, testing its sharpness. A razor-thin line of blood came up. It was ready.

"Uncle Abram, have you killed any men in the war?"

"Me? No. I've only been on merchant ships, not fighting ships. We had guns to fire at submarines. They were manned by gun crews."

"Did submarines shoot at you?"

"Yes, at two ships that I was on."

"Did they hit you?"

"One did, with torpedoes."

"Were men killed?"

"Yes, most of our crew. Twenty-two of them. I was lucky, Sorry." Abram seemed to want to end the conversation, but he continued. "War is a terrible thing, and one of the reasons I left my last ship in Eniwetok is that I didn't want to be in war anymore. I was sick of it. What I did is wrong, but I did it anyway. I thought about how much time I might have on earth, then I decided to leave." His face was cloudy.

After a few minutes of silence, broken only by the swish of the canoe through the water, the sigh of the sail, and the slight groan of the boom yoke, Sorry asked a question that had been on his mind for a long time. "What's the other world like?"

Abram looked out across the sparkling sea for a while, then said, "It's good and bad, Sorry. I saw the big cities but didn't like them. Too many people pushing and shoving, rushing around. Too much noise. Cities are dirty. They smell of automobiles and factories. You wouldn't like them."

"What are factories?" Sorry asked.

"Big buildings with smokestacks where people make things."

Sorry had seen the pictures in the Japanese magazine. "But I have to go out there someday, Uncle Abram. To the other world."

"Yes, you should," he agreed. "But then you'll come back here, as I have. Now I'll live my life away on this island. Die here, be buried here. I've seen other islands, in waters they call the Caribbean and Indian Oceans. None are as beautiful as this one . . ."

"You mean that?"

"I do. I've seen all I want of the other world. The people are greedy. They work too hard doing stupid things. They hurt each other. They do not share. Their comb is their comb. They would never think of sharing their comb. Their hat is their hat. They would never think of sharing their hat."

That was difficult to understand. If Sorry found a beautiful shell and Lokileni admired it, he would give it to her instantly.

Sorry said, "The American navy men share." By seaplane and ship they'd come back a dozen times, with clothing, food, and candy. They traded cigarettes for pandanus mats and baskets and shell necklaces. They sent a dentist, to pull teeth, and an eye doctor; they brought books in Marshallese. They brought medical supplies.

Abram said, "They should. They control all the atolls now and may never give them back. Their flag may always fly over Bikini."

"You don't like them?"

Uncle Abram shrugged. "We must be careful. The Germans and the Japanese didn't do us any favors. The Americans can give us candy and cigarettes but take away the land. Juda must tell them we can't be bought."

Sorry had never heard anyone talk the confident way his uncle did, but Abram had spent a lot of time in the *ailiñkan* and was a self-educated man, wise like Jonjen. He knew things. The island was lucky to have Uncle Abram, Tara Malolo, and Jonjen.

As soon as they reached the deep waters of the Roj-kora barrier reef, Abram positioned himself in the bow, holding the harpoon. Sorry steered with the sweep oar under his right armpit and held a string of coconut shells against the side of the canoe, just above the waterline. The bottom shell rested at the surface of the sea; the others rattled hollowly against the side of the boat. The sounds invited sharks to come up and investigate. How proud he was to be steering and handling the rattles for Abram!

They tacked back and forth. The sea outside the lagoon was almost as calm as the waters inside, with long, smooth, glistening rollers passing under them. The *clunk* of the coconut shells, the slight slap of the sail, and the muffled drum of the rollers as they hit the reef were pleasant sounds.

Abram stared intently down at the blue-green surface.

Sorry watched him, thinking how his life had changed in just two days. Abram had promised to teach him how to speak English as well as write it, play white people's games, play the guitar. Up to yesterday he hadn't quite believed all the stories about Abram Makaoliej. Now he did.

Abram suddenly murmured, "Come to me . . ."

Sorry glanced over the side. In a wide ribbon of sunlight, he saw the dim shape of a shark slide through the drifting sea particles and tiny fish.

"A tiger, but it's small," Abram said. "Keep rattling."

Fish can hear as well as smell, Sorry knew. They listen and often become curious. Sometimes, for big fish, sound is better than bait.

"Another one, also small," Abram said, and leaned out once more to look down at the water. This shark had risen higher and was plainly seven feet long, a young one. It fantailed toward the rattling, then curved away and sank back down into the depths.

"The *jimman* is down there. I can feel him," said Abram. "Rattle harder."

Sorry took another grip on the coconut twine and banged the shells harder against the side of the canoe.

After what seemed ages, Abram said softly, "Here he comes."

Sorry leaned out and his breath caught. What was beside and below them was at least fourteen or fifteen feet long, almost as long as the canoe; mottled gray, an old tiger.

Uncle Abram was now standing, bracing his knees against the sides of the outrigger, body bent slightly forward. He was aiming the harpoon, ready to drive it down. "It is the same one, Sorry. My spearhead is still in his back."

The tiger was swimming alongside and seemed to be eyeing them. He was about five feet below the clear upper surface, moving slowly, keeping pace. The body was so thick that Abram could not have wrapped his arms around it.

For the longest time Abram aimed the harpoon at the great back, and Sorry waited for the plunge of the steel head, the whipping of the coiled line as the monster made his first bloody run, hauling the canoe along as if it were a gull feather. They might be towed for miles.

Sorry's heart slammed as he waited. Silently, he thought, *Now, Uncle Abram, now . . .*

If the tiger suddenly decided to attack the frail boat

instead of running, they both might perish off the reef. The tail could crush them; the jaws would finish them.

He waited, wondering if the size alone had frightened his uncle.

Abram waited, poised, the muscles in his arms and back taut.

Finally, with a glance at Sorry, he lowered the harpoon and sat down, a strange look on his face. He placed the harpoon in the bottom of the canoe; the hunt was finished.

Sorry looked over the side. The fifteen-foot tiger was gone. There'd been plenty of time for his uncle to drive the spearhead into the shark. Why didn't he do it?

After a while, Abram spoke. "I couldn't, Sorry. Here he was, years older. Still alive. Did you see my spearhead sticking out of his back? He'd carried it all this time, with honor. He gave me my scar. I gave him his. We're even."

Sorry didn't understand. They'd sailed all the way to Rojkora, six miles south of Bikini. Abram had sharpened the harpoon head until it could cut wood. Hadn't he stood there, the big back only a few feet away? Was he suddenly a coward?

Reading Sorry's face, Abram smiled. "Someday, you'll understand."

———

No more was said about it all the way home.

They talked very little, in fact. Once, Abram said, "Tell me about Tara Malolo."

Sorry told him everything he knew about the teacher.

"She seems very nice," Abram said.

Sorry agreed.

Uncle Abram stayed in the bow for the rest of the trip, resting his head on his knees, sleeping part of the way.

———

Outside their house, where his mother was dyeing table mats with berry juice, Sorry told her what had happened.

She looked out across the lagoon, which was dotted with late afternoon homecoming sails. She seemed to be making a decision of her own. Finally, she said, "Come walk with me," and rose up.

"Come walk with me" was often heard on the island. It was a phrase that sought privacy, a way of being able to talk without being overheard: a way to say special and important things.

Past the Ijjirik dwelling, where no other ears could hear her, she said, "I have the strangest feeling that my brother has come home to die."

That was in the Marshallese tradition, of course. Die on your home island. Off Rojkora, Abram had said he'd die here. Did he mean soon?

Sorry was stunned. He looked so healthy.

"The first thing he does is go after the tiger shark to settle an old battle . . ."

Sorry nodded.

"He brought a big bottle of pills with him. I can't read the words on it, but I know it came from London. He carries a smaller bottle of them in his pants pocket."

Abram ill? Come home to die? That was hard to believe.

"Have you asked him about it?"

Mother Rinamu shook her head, frowning at the idea. "You never ask that kind of question. It is too personal." She added, "Don't say anything to anyone. I might be wrong . . ."

Sorry nodded. He would keep quiet. Yet he knew he would continue to worry.

On August 6, 1945, the *Enola Gay*, a U.S. Army Air Force B-29 bomber, released Little Boy over the city of Hiroshima, Japan. Every building within 4,000 yards of the explosion was destroyed. The death count was estimated at over 200,000, including those who died later.

12

Uncle Abram had listened to the news broadcasts from Kwajalein over the U.S. Armed Forces Radio Network and made notes each evening since a few days after he'd returned home over a year ago. He'd repaired the powerful Japanese radio set in the barracks building. A small gas engine powered the generator and fed electricity to big batteries. The broadcasts were in English.

That was the way he'd learned to speak and write English, he told Sorry. Just by listening to the radio. It was a good way to learn. He'd done it on merchant ships when he was off duty, going to the radio room. Operators helped him with the writing and with the meanings of words. Sorry decided he'd do the same thing—listen and ask Abram about the words he didn't understand.

So at around sunset each day, he went to the council place, and almost everyone in the village sat in a circle to listen eagerly to Abram Makaoliej relate the news. A miraculous event. Mothers and babies and men Jonjen's age and women Yolo's age, everyone, went to listen. No longer did they need to wait for an outrigger from Eniwetok or Rongelap for news from the *ailiñ-kan*. The outside world had become accessible.

At first, everyone went to see and hear the amazing

radio, crowding into the wooden building or standing outside it. But they soon realized they could not understand a single word. So Chief Juda decided it would be better for the islanders to go to the council place later and let Abram repeat, in Marshallese, what he'd just heard. The people talked for hours after each broadcast.

Sorry usually went with Abram to the barracks.

This August evening, Abram turned on the black box with its brass dials, warming it up for a few seconds. Then his body jolted forward. His eyes grew wide. His forehead bunched in a frown. His hard hands grasped the radio table until his knuckles turned white.

"What is it, Uncle Abram?" Sorry asked.

Abram held up a hand for silence, slowly shaking his head as if to deny the news. He was making notes.

"What is it?" Sorry asked again.

Abram waved his hand angrily, demanding silence.

A few minutes later, he swiveled around, his face grave. He said slowly, almost in disbelief, "The Americans have invented a terrible new bomb. They dropped it on Hiroshima, a city in Japan, this morning. The Japanese are saying that thousands are dead. The whole city has been destroyed. One bomb. Just one bomb . . ."

Sorry knew about bombs from the war talk of the last three years. "What kind of bomb?" he asked.

"An atom bomb . . ."

Atom? "What is that?"

Uncle Abram shook his head and the next words came out in bewildered pauses while he looked at his notes. "It doesn't use gunpowder . . . It uses nuclear fission . . . whatever that is . . . The heat was over three hundred thousand degrees . . . The cloud from it went up fifty thousand feet . . . People were turned into ashes in a split second . . . Those who didn't die instantly were blinded . . . It sounds like a bomb to end the world . . ."

"One bomb did all that? Killed thousands? . . ."

"Even the announcer didn't understand how it worked. He said it was a highly guarded secret. Only a few people knew about it." Abram stopped, as if trying to think through what had happened. "The American president said the bomb was dropped only to force Japan to surrender . . ."

"Have they done that?"

"I don't know." Abram just sat there numbly, saying nothing.

A few minutes later, just past sunset, the people of Bikini Atoll, on their mats in the council place, learned of the atomic bomb.

The lagoon was calm, lit with gold bounced from beneath the horizon. Gold lined the bottoms of the towering clouds to the west. The air was still. The tiny island was at complete and blessed peace. Sorry could not really understand what had happened in the sky over Hiroshima. No one else could, either, including Abram.

At *kejota*, the evening meal, Sorry asked Tara, "Do you think the Americans are happy about all those people dying?" There was confusion on his face and in his eyes. He couldn't imagine that many people losing their lives instantly, with no warning.

Tara frowned at the question. Finally, slowly, she said, "If you had a son or daughter or brother or sister who had been killed by the Japanese, then you might not be unhappy."

78

"War is a very personal thing," said Abram. "Some of our own Marshallese people were killed on Eniwetok, Kwajalein, Jaluit, Roi, and Namur when the Americans attacked. They weren't soldiers. They died just the same."

"And on Majuro, too," Tara added. She'd gone to college there, of course.

Sorry had never thought of war as being personal. He knew the soldiers killed each other without knowing each other. He'd never thought much beyond that fact. He'd never thought about their families.

"Most of those people in Hiroshima were not soldiers, were they?" Sorry asked.

"I'm sure they weren't," Tara said.

"They were just like us," his mother said.

Like us, he thought. *Sitting there innocently like us. Jonjen and Yolo and Lokileni and Abram and Tara Malolo and my mother and myself. Suddenly, all dead. Burned alive or blown to bits.*

"The old days, when we used the big clamshells for axes, were better," Jonjen said. "It was hand-to-hand. No bombs."

Abram said, "Yes, Grandfather, they were better. The best . . ."

No one wanted to talk further about all the dead in Hiroshima, and silence fell around the cookhouse.

After the meal, Sorry crossed the ravine and went for a walk along the barrier reef in the early darkness. On some walks, he'd felt close to his father and had shouted questions into the sea roar and wind. This night he had no questions that his father could answer.

Later, on his sleeping mat, he dreamed about the explosion in the sky, the fireball that Abram had described, and woke up screaming.

Three days later, Abram told everyone that another terrible bomb had been dropped, this time on Nagasaki, Japan. He said an estimated 140,000 people had been killed.

Sorry could not understand why it was necessary for so many innocent people to die once again.

Then, on August 14, Abram announced that Japan had surrendered. Sorry joined in the cheers of joy. The world war was over.

Book 11
Crossroads

Plans for the postwar atom bomb tests, Operation Crossroads, had begun in secrecy during October 1945. Officers in the Special Weapons Division of Naval Operations started searching for a place on which to drop an aerial bomb, then somewhere to explode one underwater. A few days before Christmas 1945, Bikini lagoon was chosen by the U.S. Navy as the target for the world's fourth and fifth atomic explosions. The islanders had no idea they were about to become famous overnight.

1

Early in February 1946, a large U.S. ship with a strange-looking bow—a bow that looked to Sorry like the bill of a storm petrel—came mysteriously into the lagoon and dropped anchor.

Abram was still asleep. Lately he hadn't seemed as lively as before. Sorry thought maybe the disease, if indeed there was one, had begun to take its toll. He'd mentioned as much to his mother and she agreed.

Though the ship put boats into the water, no one came ashore. The boats went off in several directions. Painted the usual U.S. Navy gray, the ship sat out on the horizon, and curiosity among the islanders grew by the minute. After anchoring, officers usually landed quickly to pay their respects to Chief Juda.

Along with many others, Sorry and Lokileni watched for almost an hour. Then Sorry went to awaken Abram.

"There's a navy ship out in the lagoon but it hasn't sent a boat in," Sorry said.

"Maybe they're just slow today," Abram said tiredly.

Because he could speak English, Abram had become the island's interpreter to the navy. Whenever there was a problem, a need to communicate, Abram was the spokesman.

Sorry waited while Abram pulled on a pair of dungarees and a shirt, then they launched a canoe and went out to investigate.

The USS *Sumner* had guns fore and aft, a single stack, and two masts. Abram said it was the oldest navy ship he'd ever seen. Despite the guns, it didn't appear to be a fighting ship.

They pulled up alongside the gangway and tied up to the float. The young officer stationed there seemed surprised to hear Abram ask, in good English, about the purpose of their visit.

The ensign replied, "We're going to take soundings to determine the depth of the lagoon, then blow up any large coral heads."

"Why?" Abram asked. Sorry wished he could understand all the words. He'd made a lot of progress over the last two years, but the men were talking too rapidly for him to follow the conversation.

"I don't really know," the ensign replied. "But I'll make a guess that we'll probably update the Japanese charts. Indicate depths, any hazards."

"Is that necessary?"

"I guess it is," the ensign said.

Abram thanked him, and soon their canoe was heading toward the beach.

Chief Juda was waiting to question them. A large group of villagers stood near him.

"I think they're up to something," Abram said, and explained what the officer had told him.

"If I were you, Juda, I'd try to find out exactly why they're here. This is still our island."

Everyone looked at the gray ship again, puzzled by it and the need for soundings.

"I don't want to cause trouble," said Juda.

Sorry spoke up. "Chief, he's just asking you to find out."

"Quiet, boy!" barked Leje Ijjirik, who resented Sorry's presence on the council.

"I'm not a boy any longer," Sorry shot back. Leje had not liked his father.

Abram, eyeing Leje, said, "He has a right to his opinion."

"Ha," said Leje.

The impromptu meeting on the beach broke up.

Early on the third morning after the *Sumner* arrived, a dynamite blast shattered the lagoon quiet.

Abram was asleep again. Sorry and Lokileni launched a canoe and sailed out to where the water had erupted. Over what had been a coral head they found dead fish. The big coral head had disappeared. Soon there was another explosion.

After that day, four of the ship's large boats, dragging cables behind them, sailed every morning. They were on a precise course, Sorry noticed. They hunted for coral heads, plotting them, and then the dynamite divers took over.

In addition to blasting the coral, the Americans planted buoys. As the dry, hot days went by, the villagers saw an amphibious boat crawl up on the beach each morning, usually piled high with steel girders and welding gear.

With others, Sorry and Lokileni squatted in the sand and watched in awe as an eighty-foot steel-pipe navigational beacon was erected, welding sparks flashing blue, cascading downward. Sorry had never seen a welding torch and had to ask Abram about it. Sailors swung around the beacon like monkeys.

Many were tall men, blond and blue eyed—so different from Sorry—white bodies bronzed by the Pacific sun. He felt small and insignificant watching them, wishing he'd been born in their land.

No one was prepared for what was happening on the island and all over the lagoon. From just the one ship had come a whirlwind of activity. Her boats cut white wakes across the water and her sailors swarmed ashore to erect other towers, each taking a day or two.

Still, no one knew why the *Sumner* sailors were working ashore and all over the blue-green waters. The sailors didn't seem to know either. A secret, one said.

Abram ventured a guess. "They're turning our lagoon into a harbor."

"Can they do that?" Sorry asked.

They could, without asking Juda or anyone else. Tara said, "The American flag is flying over the island, just like the Japanese flag flew over it; before that, the German flag; before the Germans, the Spanish flag . . . They can do anything they want."

Bikini had been selected because the weather there was generally good and the atoll offered a large lagoon with shallow-water anchorage areas and islands for support facilities. It was within a thousand miles of a bomber base and was more than five hundred miles from the nearest cities and ship and aircraft routes.

2

On the second Sunday in February, just before the morning church services ended, Sorry watched as a navy Catalina flying boat glided out of the sky and landed about a quarter mile from the beach. It motored closer, propellers flashing in the sun.

Visiting aircraft were no longer a novelty, but as always, curiosity about who was coming ashore, and for what reason, sent the islanders to the water's edge. The church emptied.

A yellow rubber raft soon appeared at the side of the aircraft, and two men in khaki uniforms climbed into it. Another man wore a white shirt and blue trousers. He was obviously Marshallese.

Then another raft slid out of the aircraft. Two more navy men, plus another Marshallese, got into that one. Soon the outboards were disturbing the Sunday quiet.

Over the six months since the bombing of Hiroshima and Nagasaki and the surrender of Japan, only three or four flying boats had visited, the navy men on them staying ashore for several hours, taking photographs, saying that they just wanted to look around.

Abram said, watching the approaching rafts, "I have an uneasy feeling. I've had it ever since that ship anchored out there. The Americans are much too interested in this island. They want something."

"What could they want?" Sorry asked. The war was long over.

"I think we'll find out very soon," Abram said.

Chief Juda walked down to the water as the rafts powered up on the sand.

Looking at the occupants of the second raft, Abram said, "Uh-oh." The Marshallese man wore a new navy khaki shirt and trousers, with black shoes. He was maybe in his sixties and had iron gray hair. As soon as his feet touched the sand, he said to Juda, loud enough for everyone else to hear, "I am Jeimata."

They had heard of Jeimata—of lush Ailinglapalap—but had never seen him. He was paramount chief of the Ralik chain, ruler of the northern Marshalls; owner, he claimed, of all the islands, including Bikini. Why had the navy brought him here?

Everyone watched as Juda bowed slightly and shook hands with him. Sorry knew, at that moment, that Juda was afraid of him. Jeimata's eyes were the eyes of a mako, cold as the ocean a mile down.

Abram said quietly, "The navy will use him. Juda must be careful."

Sorry asked himself, *What do they want? What do they want? . . .*

The oldest naval officer, with white hair poking out from under his cap, shook hands with Juda and introduced the other officers through the interpreter, who'd ridden in the first boat. The interpreter said his name was Azakel, of Kwajalein; unlike most Marshallese, he was almost chubby. The Americans must have been feeding him well since they captured the Marshalls. He wore new sunglasses, which would be worth a thousand coconuts in trade.

Azakel said, "Commodore Wyatt would like to talk to you and the people, Chief Juda. Commodore Wyatt is the military governor of the Marshalls, a very important man."

Uncle Abram had been right, Sorry thought. The Americans wanted something.

Juda nodded and pointed toward an area beneath the palms.

As everyone began walking in that direction, Abram said, "You see, Sorry, we go from being ruled by the Japanese to being ruled by the Americans."

Once they reached the palms, the governor spoke to Azakel, saying, "Everyone should sit down."

In Marshallese, Abram said to the people, "You see, the government men remain on their feet so they can be superior. It has been that way too many years. We should all keep standing. Don't sit down."

Azakel looked at Sorry's uncle with alarm, astonished that he could understand English.

Yet everyone except Abram and Sorry sat down meekly, as they'd done in the presence of white men or prominent Marshallese for years. Not too long ago, but before Sorry's lifetime, women had duckwalked when around men of importance like the governor.

There was tension in the air, caused by Abram. It was like the hushed minutes before a thunderstorm struck. Sorry looked around at the other families. Their faces were blank, waiting for words from the mighty white Americans who had delivered the atoll from the Japanese.

Abram remained standing, staring at the governor. Deep distrust was in his eyes.

With a grunt, Grandfather Jonjen got back to his feet, lifted his chin, and stood beside Abram and Sorry, planting his cane in the sand defiantly. Then Tara joined Jonjen, studying the governor, too.

Finally the governor spoke, and Azakel, after a pause, said, "You know about the atom bomb?"

Juda said, "Yes, we know," glancing at Abram. All heads turned to look at Sorry's uncle.

The governor spoke again and Azakel said, "The Americans must now test this weapon in a different way, and Bikini has been chosen as the atoll for these necessary tests."

So that's why the Sumner is in the lagoon, Sorry thought.

Abram shouted, "No!" and the people turned to look at him again. They had been startled by his loud cry. He was glaring at the governor.

Juda said, "Let Azakel finish."

Abram shouted again, in English this time, directly to the governor. "No atom bomb here. Look what it did to Hiroshima!"

Then Sorry's mother pleaded with her brother. "Please, Abram, please sit down and let him finish."

The governor and all the other officers and Jeimata were frowning at Abram. They had not expected to find anyone on Bikini like Abram Makaoliej.

Sorry immediately thought of the albatross that had moaned when it passed Nantil two years ago. *This was what the bird had been moaning about. The atom bomb.*

Translating again, Azakel said, "It will be done for peace and security around the world."

"Whose peace and security?" Abram yelled in Marshallese, then in English.

The governor took a deep breath and spoke again.

Azakel said, "Many warships will be anchored in the lagoon. The tests will find out how well the ships will survive in future attacks."

The *ailiñkan* had come to Bikini once again, Sorry thought. First the Spaniards, then the Germans and the Japanese. Now the nice Americans, first offering candy, then the atom bomb.

"There are atolls where no people live," Abram said distinctly, both in English and in Marshallese.

"But none with a lagoon this large or this deep," Azakel argued.

That wasn't true. Kwajalein's lagoon was much larger and deeper, Sorry had heard.

Azakel said forcefully, "The Americans have flown everywhere. It has to be a place free of storms, where the wind blows in one direction and where the sea currents avoid fishing grounds and inhabited islands, an area where whales do not travel."

Sorry remembered that Abram had told the people about the poison that came from the bomb and made everyone sick. Radiation! It could come through air or water. "Let the Americans fly some more and find another place," Abram said in both languages. His hands were clenched into fists; rage showed around his mouth.

The navy officers looked at the paramount chief for help. Jeimata said stonily to Juda, "Make him be quiet."

Juda looked as if he wanted the sand to swallow him up. He said weakly, "Please, Abram . . ." He glanced toward Sorry's mother for help. Her expression didn't change.

The governor took a deep breath and tried to ignore the troublemaker, speaking again. Azakel interpreted. "They will move everyone and all of your possessions; provide new houses, provide you with food—"

"Don't listen to him!" Abram shouted in Marshallese.

"Be quiet, Abram," said Leje Ijjirik.

"You can return here in several years," continued Azakel, translating. "Everything will be restored to the way it is this morning."

Sorry could see that Azakel was sweating. His brown skin had a reddish tinge.

"Liar!" Abram shouted at the governor. He was trembling with anger. "The bomb will poison our earth, kill our trees, poison our lagoon. No coconuts, no fish—"

Juda said, "Please let us listen to them."

Abram shouted, *"Letao!"* Liar!

Sorry echoed him.

The governor raised his palms in a gesture of peace and then began to talk slowly, Azakel translating just as slowly. In another tongue, the governor sounded like Jonjen preaching.

"You are like the children of Israel, whom the Lord saved from the enemy and then led into the Promised Land. We have saved you from the enemy by making the bomb, and now for the good of mankind and to end all wars forever, we must experiment with it. We've searched the world over and know that Bikini is the best place for the tests."

Azakel matched the governor in word and tone.

Chief Juda finally said to Azakel, "We will talk about

it," and the interpreter motioned to the Americans that they should leave for a while.

Abram snorted to the villagers. " 'Children of Israel'? They have rehearsed that speech. They know the right words to use."

Once the officers and Azakel had moved away, Abram said to the people, "They aren't telling you the truth. I've listened to the radio all these months and heard about the terrible sickness of Hiroshima that comes with the atom bomb. The scientists don't even know how long the poison lasts. It could be a thousand years."

Juda reminded, "The governor said *several* years."

"They don't know. *They do not know, Chief Juda.* The news broadcasts have said they don't know. Do you think I made this up?"

Jonjen said, "I am against this atom bomb. It kills people and I am against any killing."

Chief Jeimata said, "Do as the Americans ask. I order you to do as the Americans ask."

Abram said, unafraid of the Ralik ruler, "You don't live here!"

Jeimata's face darkened.

There was argument for more than an hour, Abram saying, "You know from the Bible that there are animals in the white man's world called sheep. They are easily led and never resist. They do not think, they just follow. They even follow each other into death. Today, you are sheep. Don't you understand?"

Sorry had heard of sheep and understood what Abram was saying.

Tara said heatedly to those seated, "You were born here! This is your land! You don't have to give it up!

Let them find a place in America to test their bomb!"

Most of the time the people listened to the teacher. Abram glanced over at her with appreciation in his eyes.

Leje Ijjirik said, "They just want to use the lagoon for a while. What harm is that? I think they will pay us much money, then we'll come back in two years and everything will be the same. They will give us many things, as they have already done."

Abram shouted, "I didn't hear them offer to pay anything, just move us!"

Chief Juda said quietly, "They will pay us, I'm sure."

Abram said, "Ask them!"

Finally, sighing, Juda said, "We must vote. They are waiting."

Nine *alab*s voted for nine families to move. Sorry and Jonjen cast a vote against; one Makaoliej family, to which Abram belonged, voted against. It all occurred in less than an hour.

Juda sent an Ijjirik girl to summon the Americans back to the meeting place and then said to them, "If the United States government and the scientists of the world want to use our atoll for further development which, with God's blessings, will result in kindness and benefit to all mankind, my people will be pleased to go elsewhere for a while."

Sorry thought, *Poor Chief Juda. He is not accustomed to dealing with authorities.*

Abram said bitterly, "You've made a great mistake, Juda. You've made a great mistake."

As Azakel translated, the governor congratulated Juda and thanked the people, saying he was certain everyone would like their new home, that the navy and the U.S. government would do everything humanly possible to help them resettle.

Tara took Abram's hand and said, "You tried . . ."

He sighed. "But I didn't win."

Sorry looked at the faces of the villagers sitting there on the matting. They did not know what had happened to them in less than two hours. A few were frowning, but most faces were blank as the governor and his staff hurried back to their rafts.

———

Sorry sat side by side with Abram in the sand and watched as the blue Catalina built up speed and lifted off the lagoon, heading west again. His mother and Lokileni sat a few feet away, near Tara, Jonjen, and Yolo. No one was speaking. Sorry was proud that he'd voted against the white men and their bomb.

The other villagers watched in silence, too, standing in little family groups as the seaplane disappeared. As the afternoon went by, Sorry thought he sensed remorse setting in, and a sudden sadness. Slowly, slowly, all the fine words about them being the children of Israel led to the Promised Land, and how the bomb drop would result in kindness and benefit to all mankind, sank in. Some of the people now realized they'd voted to leave their place of birth, to have their dwellings torn down, to have the island destroyed, to go live on another island, which they'd probably never seen and probably knew nothing about.

Tara said, "The Americans didn't say where we'd be sent."

At last, Abram sighed. "You know, our people agreed to this just because the white men asked them to. They don't know it yet but they'll leave behind the most important thing of all—home."

He seemed worn down as well as sad. Lifeless. *Was* he ill?

"Do you know what happened here? We see the Americans as so great and powerful that we can't say no to them, and the governor used our belief in God against us. I cry for our people, Sorry. They think they'll be back in a few years and everything will be the same. It won't, Sorry. It won't ever be the same. Once that bomb is dropped it will never be the same here. They lied to Juda and to all of us."

Sorry said thoughtfully, "Uncle Abram, why is it that the Americans want to test bombs when the war is over? Isn't the outside world at peace now?"

"I don't think it's quite that simple. America still has enemies."

"Why can't everyone live in peace, the way we used to have it here?"

"Sorry, if I could answer that question, I'd be the most important man on earth."

Ruta Rinamu nodded in agreement.

"Well, how can we stop the test? What can we do?" Sorry asked.

"Yes," Tara said. "What can we do?" Jonjen echoed her.

Abram thought awhile. "I'm not sure. Something, perhaps. When I was a seaman, I learned about strikes. Do you know what a strike is?"

Sorry shook his head.

"A strike is when workers fight back against bad treatment, low wages. They refuse to work; they protest."

"Can we do that?"

"I don't think it would do any good to strike. But we can protest. That means 'fight against.' In the other world, there are many newspapers and magazines and radio stations. If we can get to them in time, maybe we can force the navy to make another choice, find another atoll without people on it."

"What are the chances, Uncle Abram?"

Abram took a long time to answer.

"Not very good."

Then silence fell upon them again.

Vice Admiral William H. P. Blandy, commander of Operation Crossroads, told the international press that the Bikinians could be returned to their island in a matter of months.

3

Heart thudding, Sorry sat strapped in, life jacketed, along with Chief Juda, Abram, Jeton Kejibuki, and Manoj Ijjirik, who held tightly to the seat piping, eyes closed. The engine noise mounted to a fury, and the seaplane began its takeoff run across the lagoon, slamming into low waves until it rose into the air.

All the other members of the council had refused to go, frightened by the white man's flying machine. The navy had offered to fly Juda and the council in search of a suitable island to temporarily replace Bikini as home. A four-engine aircraft, larger than the usual Catalinas, was being used.

Once they were in the air, Sorry began to breathe easier. His heartbeat slowed. Never in his life had he thought he'd be sitting in a roaring, vibrating airplane.

Soon the sailor in the cabin told him he could remove his seat belt and look out one of the window ports. Below were the sea and drifting clouds, a new and exciting view of them.

A naval officer, pudgy, red-haired, freckle-faced Lieutenant Hastings, the military governor's representative, accompanied them. He shouted above the engine pound, "We'll go to Ujae and Lae first."

The plane finally swooped low over Ujae and Lae, islands much smaller than Bikini. The people there waved as the winged shadow rumbled across their sands and palms.

Sorry still couldn't believe he was actually up in the sky, and now enjoying it. But Chief Juda, whose face was almost milk white, sat grasping the seat-frame pipes.

Abram said in English to Hastings, "The council decided against any island that is already inhabited."

Juda, vomiting into a bag hurriedly given to him, finally gasped, "Rongerik." He'd been told that Rongerik, 120 miles east of Bikini, had no residents.

The name, for some reason, bothered Sorry. Long ago, he had heard bad things about the island from Yolo, and 120 miles seemed halfway around the world to him.

Abram said that the navy really didn't care where they went, just so long as they soon left Bikini with their pandanus mats, outriggers, chickens, and dogs. It was up to them to select a new island.

Jeton Kejibuki was also sick and throwing up. Sorry himself felt a little queasy as the plane drummed on for another two hours. Then it descended a bit and Lieutenant Hastings, coming back from the cockpit, said, "Rongerik."

Chief Juda staggered out of his seat to look down.

"Do you want to land?" Lieutenant Hastings asked, and Abram interpreted for Juda, who shook his head.

"We should land," Abram said, but Juda refused.

To Sorry, the atoll, much smaller than Bikini, did not look too bad. There weren't as many palm trees or pandanus, but the beach of the main island was wider than Bikini's.

102

Sorry saw sudden tears in Manoj Ijjirik's eyes; Jeton Kejibuki stared down at the aircraft floor. Abram was clearly frustrated. They were all unhappy with Juda's decision not to land.

Sorry took another look below. The lagoon was less than half the size of Bikini's, and some of the islands in the ring were mostly bare sand or low brush with vines on them.

"Go home, go home," Juda said weakly to Abram, and Abram, in turn, told the lieutenant.

Juda sat with his head down, defeated.

"It is not a good island!" Abram shouted to him over the thunder of the engines.

Juda didn't even raise his head to answer.

———

The villagers gathered expectantly a few minutes after the plane landed, and they waited for the rubber boats to bring Chief Juda and his party to the beach.

Face still pale, Juda climbed out and walked unsteadily toward the people.

"What happened?" asked Jonjen.

"We decided on Rongerik, where no one lives."

"I've heard bad things about Rongerik. That's why no one lives there," said Jonjen.

"It's temporary; we'll be home again in two years," Juda said. "That's what the navy has promised."

Two years is a very long time, Sorry thought.

Jonjen demanded, "Why didn't you go to more islands, south of here?"

"Because I knew everyone wanted to stay as near home as possible. We already know that almost every atoll south of here is too small or is inhabited."

Standing at the back of the group, Abram said

quietly and sadly, "Juda, I don't think this island will be our home again for a long, long time, if ever. It will be poisoned by the bombs."

Leje Ijjirik turned swiftly toward Abram with annoyance, shouting, "We've heard what you said before! We're very tired of hearing it. We'll benefit by leaving here. The navy will give us money sooner or later. They'll take good care of us on Rongerik. They'll give us food and medicine. They have doctors."

That was like Leje, Sorry thought. He would argue with a goony bird.

"Wait until you see Rongerik, Leje! Just wait!" Abram shouted back, his face stormy.

They'd always been such gentle people, seldom raising their voices to each other. Now there was dark tension in the air. Villager against villager.

"You are crazy, Abram! You are insane!" Leje shouted, raising a fist.

"He is telling the truth, Leje," Tara said loudly. "I've been to Rongerik. I was born eighteen miles away. Remember?"

There was murmuring in the crowd, then the meeting broke up. Most of the people went unhappily back to their houses. Only Leje and a few others were still pleased about the week-old decision to leave Bikini. Sorry believed most villagers had already changed their minds and wished they were staying.

Lokileni said, her thin face dark with anger, "Uncle Abram isn't crazy."

Leje ignored her and walked away.

Outraged, Ruta Rinamu called loudly after him, "My brother is not crazy!"

Abram stood silently, an odd expression on his face.

There was a grayish tone to it now, over the brown. He did not look well.

"Are you all right?" Sorry asked.

His mother repeated worriedly, "Abram, are you all right?"

He took two pills out of the small bottle that was in his pocket and placed them under his tongue. "I'm all right," he said, taking a deep breath.

Elderly Jibiji Kejibuki, trying to soothe tempers, said to Abram, "Tell us about Rongerik."

Abram finally nodded. "The main island is not nearly as large as this one. The lagoon is probably less than a quarter the size of ours. It is a very meager atoll. Leje is wrong about the money. The navy offered to move us into temporary houses away from the island. That's all they offered. Nothing else. I understood every word the governor said, and he never mentioned money."

Abram suddenly seemed exhausted and sat down on a palm bole. Sorry and his mother exchanged looks.

———

At the evening meal, Lokileni repeated, "Rongerik," to herself, as if learning a new foreign word. Nothing soft or musical about it, Sorry realized. *Bikini* was musical, he thought.

Abram, who had been mostly silent since the afternoon meeting, finally spoke about the day. "All the way back here Manoj and I talked about making the navy find another island, letting us keep this one. Juda opened his mouth only once. 'We are so small and they are so large,' he said. That's true, but I know one thing: We gave up without a fight. We could have said no.

Maybe nothing would have changed, but we could have said no."

"Were there any schools of fish?" Sorry's mother asked.

"Not many," Sorry admitted. "But we did see some tuna break water."

Without fish, they'd starve.

Juda had ordered the women to start making roofing and wall panels tomorrow, the men to strip the pandanus trees of all mature leaves to take to Rongerik. Grandmother Yolo and Lokileni would help with the plaiting; Sorry would strip leaves.

"And pandanus on the other islands?" his mother asked.

"Not very many. The atoll is shaped like the palm of my hand." He added, "As if that makes any difference."

"We can survive for two years." She was always optimistic.

"Can't we call another meeting?" Sorry asked.

"Yes, but the navy might not show up," Abram replied.

Jonjen said, " 'God will be pleased if you move,' the governor told us. How could the navy know what pleases God?"

———

Later in the evening Sorry sat with Lokileni, Abram, and Tara on the beach in front of their dwelling. The lights of the *Sumner* cut the velvet curtain of darkness over the lagoon. That old ship was a constant reminder of what was going to happen. When the wind was blowing onshore, her loudspeakers could be heard, with sailors' shrill piping or recordings of reveille or taps.

The villagers could not escape the sounds. Less than a month ago only the surf and cries of unseen birds were carried on the night wind.

"Uncle Abram, you said you had a plan."

"I do," he answered quietly, eyes focused on the *Sumner's* lights.

"What is it?" Sorry asked, looking at his uncle's profile in the pale moonlight.

Abram didn't answer for the longest time, then said, "I'll tell you later."

"You heard Grandfather Jonjen say Yolo wouldn't go because of Libokra," Lokileni said.

Abram laughed softly. "That silly tale. Yolo will be slung across somebody's shoulder like she's a sack of spider lilies. The navy won't leave an old woman here to watch the bombs go off."

Long ago, according to island legend, an evil spirit named Libokra stole Rongerik from the southern atolls and placed it in the north. She tried to steal Bikini but was chased away by a friendly spirit, Orijabato, and finally had to settle on Rongerik. She was murdered on a stormy night and her body was thrown into the lagoon, poisoning all the sea life. After her death, the coconuts and pandanus clusters were fewer and smaller; water in the few shallow wells tasted strange and caused sickness. No one had lived on Rongerik for years, supposedly because of Libokra.

"That's pure nonsense," Tara said. "But I admit that my people don't visit Rongerik very often. And never at night."

"Is that when the dead witch flies around?" Lokileni asked.

"Believe it if you want," Tara said, laughing.

"If it's all nonsense, why doesn't anyone live there?" Sorry asked.

"I don't know," Tara admitted.

Abram said, "Simply because it's a worthless atoll. I heard that years ago. Why people won't live there has nothing to do with Libokra, whatever Yolo thinks."

Grandmother Yolo was more than half-crazy, Sorry often thought. She had been that way before Sorry was born. But he still loved her.

He'd done something terrible to her when he was six or seven and still regretted it. She never wanted to look at herself, afraid she'd see a spirit. So he borrowed a piece of mirror from Manoj Ijjirik's house and waited until she was sound asleep in the afternoon, then held it about two feet above her face and woke her up. She saw herself and screamed. His father chased him far up the beach.

There was a big barrier beach rock that Yolo usually sat on. There she would be, stiff backed with her eyes closed, hands on her knees. Once Sorry asked her what she was listening to. Her eyes moved around under the lids and her toothless chin worked. That was when she would still talk. She told him she was listening to voices from the ocean, all the people who had died off of the barrier beach for a hundred years. For a while, he really thought she heard them.

Had she talked to his father? She wouldn't say.

What began as a few Pentagon orders in early January 1946, had become a paper flood that would eventually involve more than 250 ships; over 150 aircraft; 42,000 personnel; 25,000 Geiger radiation counters; hundreds of still and motion picture cameras. Approximately 160 journalists from around the world would soon be headed for Bikini.

4

With the early sun again climbing to erase the night's dew and the usual fluffy clouds adrift over the far horizon, Sorry and Abram sailed the Eniwetok canoe out to the USS *Sumner*.

After asking permission, they tied up alongside the wooden landing pontoon. Sorry didn't know the reason for the visit, and Abram hadn't volunteered any information.

There were times when Sorry's uncle was as open as the sea and sky; other times he closed himself off like a clam. This morning he was a clam.

Abram spoke to the petty officer in charge of the gangway watch. He asked to see the chief boatswain. The bo'sun always bossed the deck crew and was responsible for deck maintenance.

"For what reason?" asked the sailor.

"We're going to tear down several buildings, and I need some red paint to mark the supports we'll take to Rongerik."

Abram later told Sorry what had been said at the gangway.

Lieutenant Hastings had decided it would be best if both the church and the council-school buildings were dismantled and transported to the new island. Both were part of community life and might help ward off homesickness. The lieutenant had promised Juda that the navy would cooperate in every way.

The sailor shrugged and said into the loudspeaker system, "Chief bo'sun to the quarterdeck! Chief bo'sun to the quarterdeck." The bo'sun was always in charge of the paint locker.

Sorry looked along the length of the gray, riveted hull, wishing he could board it; see, up close, all the things on the white man's ship. He could smell food being prepared and wondered what the sailors would eat this day. The smells were completely different from those that came from the beach fire pits.

Soon a stocky man appeared, yellow hair poking from under his hat and from the V of his short-sleeved khaki shirt, tattoos on his arms. With a frown, he asked, "Who wants me?"

The gangway-watch sailor indicated Abram, standing barefooted and bare chested on the pontoon in his rolled-up dungarees, displaying a warm smile.

Puzzled, the chief bo'sun looked from Abram to Sorry in the canoe. He muttered, "Yeah?"

Abram repeated what he'd told the gangway sailor: The paint was needed for marking.

"How much?"

"Ten gallons and two brushes, please."

"Give you five." Then the chunky yellow-haired man paused and scratched his head. "Oh, what the hell, I'll give you ten. This old tub's gonna go out of duty once we hit Norfolk. Then to a scrap yard. Why should I care?"

He started to turn away, and Abram, ever polite, called up, "Sir, these are for you."

Behind his back, he'd been holding two dye-decorated pandanus mats, the work of Sorry's mother.

"Hey, thank you," said the chief bo'sun as Abram passed them up.

Abram said, "If you come ashore, I'll treat you to some palm wine."

———

A seaman appeared carrying two five-gallon cans of red lead, a primer used on all navy ships, eased down the steep gangway, and handed them to Abram, along with two brushes.

"What are you going to paint?" Sorry asked. To put a mark on supports didn't require ten gallons. It required a brushful.

"You'll find out in time."

A moment later, the outrigger was heading back for the beach. "I think we're in business with the U.S. Navy," Abram said.

"What does that mean?" Sorry asked.

"That means we may find out more about the bomb. That lieutenant isn't going to tell us. No officer is. But the enlisted men may talk. They're great, like the crewmen were on my ships."

The canoe slid on toward the island.

"But why do we need that much red paint?"

"I said I'll tell you later."

Annoyed, Sorry finally said, "Uncle Abram, I really thought you were going to make the navy find a new lagoon so we could stay here. I thought that's why we were going to the ship this morning."

"We need newspapermen. None have arrived. The radio said that many *will* arrive. Be patient. You can be sure that some will visit us on Rongerik. Then we can tell our story and come back here after they help us stop the tests."

Was that possible? Could Abram do that? He seemed to be serious. Sorry knew he'd read newspapers in the ports his ships had visited. He understood the white men's ways. Could he make them choose another atoll?

"Will there be time?" Sorry asked.

"I think so. The radio said the first test will be in late May or early June. It's only February. We have time."

Abram's words were barely out of his mouth when there was an explosion behind them. They looked toward the center of the lagoon at the misty remains of a huge spout of falling water. Another big coral cropping had been blown to clear the nine-square-mile anchorage.

Sorry said, "They're not waiting, are they?"

"No, they're not," Abram replied, staring at the drifting mist.

One of the island's outriggers was already moving toward the explosion to pick up dead fish.

Abram suddenly grimaced and grabbed at his chest, gritting his teeth. His face was contorted with pain and gray in color.

Alarmed, Sorry said, "Are you all right?"

Abram reached into his pocket for the pill case and took out two.

Sorry repeated, "Are you all right, Uncle Abram?"

Abram nodded, breathing heavily.

Eyes closed, fists clenched, he sat motionless waiting for the pain spasms to stop.

Sorry had seen this same illness once before, he remembered. Jorkan Rinamu, of the family next door, was hauling in a big fish when it happened. Jorkan, an older man, later died of heart seizure.

Abram began taking some deep breaths as the pain subsided. Finally he seemed all right again, and his skin color began to return to normal.

Sorry said, "Does that happen often?"

"More lately. But it goes away after I take the pills."

Abram studied Sorry for a moment or two, then said, "So you want to know how paint will bring newspapermen?"

Sorry nodded.

"I plan to paint this canoe and its sail red, then take it into Bikini lagoon just before the bomb is ready to drop. I hope they'll see me and decide not to drop it. Then I hope the newspaper and radio people will make something big of it. 'One Man Stops the Bomb.' I hope they'll tell the world . . ."

Sorry wondered if he was dreaming. Had he heard what he thought he'd heard? *His uncle was going to sail against the atom bomb?* Maybe Abram *was* crazy.

Abram continued, "I'll find out from the radio when the bomber will come over, the day and time. I won't get too near the main target, a battleship, but I'll be close enough for the flight crew to see me."

Sorry's head was swimming. Scary, crazy words. Was he serious? One man in a canoe against the atom bomb?

"It's the only way for us to try and stop it," Abram said. *"The only way."*

"But, Uncle Abram—"

Abram waved a hand; he'd talk no more of it. "I'll tell everyone when we get to Rongerik and paint the canoe. Meanwhile, the navy must not find out."

———

As the canoe, carrying the ten gallons of red paint and two brushes, slid up on the beach, Abram Makao-liej stepped out and collapsed without a word.

Sorry yelled for help, turning his uncle faceup.

He was dead.

———

Abram was buried the next morning in the village cemetery, with Grandfather Jonjen conducting the service. It was another pretty morning on the atoll, breeze rustling the palms, sun shining, sky blue.

In the tradition, village men had made the coffin overnight, and Abram was dressed in his best white shirt and pants. The village women wailed at graveside, and Sorry wept openly. A death in the small community was always a terrible loss, and everyone grieved.

Tara Malolo talked of her admiration for Abram, and Jonjen talked of his intelligence and courage. Abram had died where he wanted to die—at home.

The villagers sang, "Bound to the promised land..."

As Jonjen talked, Sorry made a decision. He would take Abram's place in the canoe and return to Bikini on the day of the atom bomb. If no one else would volunteer, he'd go alone.

Handfuls of sand were thrown into the grave by the villagers, and Sorry joined in. Then the coffin was nailed shut as the women's wailing reached a crescendo. After the coffin was lowered, flowers were tossed upon it, and Jonjen said the final prayer.

In the afternoon, Sorry and the other men went about stripping the pandanus trees of all mature leaves. They worked quietly. Normally they would have been chattering. Sorry's mind was occupied with the death of his uncle and what Abram had told him about stopping the bomb.

Lokileni, Tara, Yolo, and Mother Rinamu joined the women to help make the thatch panels. They sat in the council building on their mats. Usually there was much talk and laughter as fingers danced over the leaves. But like the men, the women were subdued this day.

A deeper pall of doubt and anxiety had settled over the village. Abram would be missed.

Five hundred scientists of all types were preparing to participate in Operation Crossroads. Never before had people known so little about the destructive forces they were about to unleash, or about the long-range consequences. Observers would include biophysicists and nuclear physicists, biologists, zoologists, geologists, seismologists, meteorologists, hematologists for blood study, roentgenologists—experts in radiation—and dozens more. Bikini Atoll, before and after the bombs, would be the most scientifically studied 245.32 square miles on earth, and the center of it all would be the blue-green lagoon.

5

After breakfast the next day, Sorry sought out Tara and said, "Come walk with me. I couldn't sleep last night."

"Neither could I," said Tara.

The usual snores in Chief Juda's house had chased her out. She was staying with his family this week. She said she'd slept most of the night in the grove.

That happened now and then to everyone. You took your mat and went two hundred feet away, hoping the palm rats wouldn't nose around. Sorry had slept in the groves sometimes because of Yolo's and Jonjen's snores.

Tara and Sorry walked north along the beach, just above the tideline, then he stopped and looked into her dark eyes. "Abram was going to paint the Eniwetok canoe red and sail it back to Bikini, hope they'd see him and not drop the bomb."

Her mouth opened, but no words came out. From what Abram had told everyone, the atom bomb was the most destructive thing on earth. You'd want to be a thousand miles away from it. Finally, she said, "Had he lost his mind?"

"He'd been thinking about how to stop the navy

ever since the military governor came here. Remember he told us about white men protesting. How and what they do. Strikes and marches that make newspaper front pages. Later he told me men have even stopped roads from being built. I had no idea he'd been thinking about painting the canoe and—" Sorry choked up.

"Why did he tell you and not me?" Tara said, frowning.

"I don't know. I don't think he planned to tell anyone until we got to Rongerik. He told me after he had the first attack in the canoe, on our way back from getting the paint from the *Sumner*."

Tara shook her head. "Why didn't he tell me?" she asked again.

"After you, I was his best friend," Sorry said.

Some villagers, of course, like Leje, didn't approve of Abram at all. They were jealous, Sorry believed.

"You know we were in love, don't you?"

"I thought so."

"Many nights, after everyone was asleep, we took long walks and talked."

"You didn't know he had heart trouble?"

"He never told me that either. That's why it was such a shock . . ."

Sorry said, "I thought about the red paint and the bomb all last night. Since he isn't here to try and stop it, I will."

"What did you say?"

"After we get to Rongerik, I'm going to paint the canoe red and sail it back here and do exactly what Abram had planned to do."

"Oh, no! No, no, no! We won't let you."

"Who is 'we'?"

"All of us, Sorry. Abram is dead and that's enough death."

"I'm going to do it, Tara," said Sorry quietly but firmly. "I am."

Nuclear scientists estimated that the heat generated at the center of the aerial blast, "Able," would measure several million degrees Fahrenheit. The outside surface of the burst was expected to be 22,000 degrees.

6

Whatever was happening with the Americans, food was still the village priority. It always had been and always would be, no matter where they moved.

Lokileni and Sorry trolled in midmorning with a bone jig, a steel hook suspended beneath a short length of bone, wired securely. Sometimes they used several strips of plain burlap to cover the hook, streaming it behind the canoe. A steady breeze pushed the outrigger at eight or nine knots, a good speed to lure a wahoo or tuna.

Game fish often attacked anything small that moved on the surface of the water. There'd be a flash of color behind the boat and the line would spill out, then jerk tight if the hook was firmly set. Glistening, the fish might leap totally out of the water in a fountain of spray.

Waiting for a strike, Sorry looked toward the village, now without the church and community buildings. They'd been taken down the day before. Even the uprights had come down. Tara was holding school in the sand, at the edge of the main palm grove. Since he had turned fourteen two years ago and become an adult, Sorry no longer attended regularly. He felt an emptiness, looking over there, and sudden, new anger at the navy for forcing them to leave. Chief Juda had been told by Lieutenant Hastings that the move to Rongerik would take place at the end of the first week in March, about two weeks away.

Maybe they should sail *all* the canoes back into Bikini lagoon just before the bomb was to drop? They could say, "Stop the bomb or kill us all—men, women, and children. You've taken our homeland, now kill us." Let the newsmen print that!

Sorry sat there thinking how he could carry Abram's plan further: they could decorate the war canoes with flowers, always the symbols of peace, put leis around their necks and wear warriors' flower headbands, and sail back into the lagoon. *The entire village could do it!*

"When will we take our house down?" Lokileni asked, looking at the shore.

"The morning we go," he said absently.

It would take less than an hour to remove the walls and bundle them up. They'd leave the older roof thatch behind. While it might seem to the white men that the villagers' dwellings were laughable, one-room pieces of vegetation, they were perfect for tropical living.

"What about the frames?" she asked.

The frames were the only permanent parts of their house.

"The navy lieutenant said they'll provide all the new wood we need. They'll make wooden floors and tent the sides, put canvas up for the roofs. I don't think we'll want their roofs. We've slept under thatch too long. Canvas holds the heat. Our houses will be like ovens." But his mind wasn't on their new house.

Lokileni said with a laugh, "We'll use their canvas for sails."

Sorry said, "Yes, that's a good idea. Use anything they give us."

Lokileni said, "And I'm not sure I want to sleep on wood, either." The mats on coral pebbles with sand beneath were just fine. "Why change for the white men?"

Yes, why change for the white men? Sorry silently agreed. *Why do anything for them that we don't have to do?*

Everyone should be back at Bikini the day they planned to drop the bomb, he thought. *They might not see one canoe. Surely they'd see eight. They'd see the women and children. That would give the radio and newspaper people something to talk about.*

A few minutes later, the pile of *sennit* fishing line that was curled on the stern of the canoe *zing*ed, then became taut and shivered as the slender body of a wahoo shot up into the air thirty yards behind them. It plunged back into the lagoon again. The fish temporarily took their minds off Rongerik.

———

With the navy busy everywhere and other ships beginning to arrive, there were changes around the atoll every day, if not every hour. The death of Abram brought about still another change; Tara became the interpreter for Chief Juda.

Her English was not as good as Abram's, though they'd talked together in that language to practice it. But she spoke and understood enough to aid Juda in dealing with Lieutenant Hastings and some of the sailors who came ashore for one reason or another.

She also became the village nightly news reporter after listening to Armed Forces Network and taking notes. And she still taught classes in the morning.

Six thousand pairs of goggles were ordered for personnel who would be nearest the Able blast. Those personnel not fitted with goggles were told to turn away from Bikini a few seconds before the bomb drop, shut their eyes, and cover their faces with an arm. Failure to obey the instructions would result in temporary blindness.

7

A civilian, Dr. John Garrison, wearing shorts and a T-shirt, feet encased in marine field shoes, jumped off a landing craft at the tideline. Three brown canvas knapsacks were draped over his right shoulder; in his right hand was a strange, long-barreled pistol. A canteen was strapped to his hip. His thick hair was gray. He wore sunglasses.

"I'm looking for a lady named Tara Malolo," he said in Marshallese to the small children who'd run out to meet the boat, hoping for candy or cookies.

Lokileni and Sorry had seen the boat approaching and walked down to join the children. They eyed the pistol.

"I'm looking for Tara Malolo," the white man repeated.

"You speak our language," Sorry said.

The man smiled. He had a nice, warm, fatherly face. "I try. I studied night and day on the train from Washington to San Francisco, then on a ship to Hawaii, and on two more ships, until I arrived here yesterday. I was told on the *Sumner* to contact Tara Malolo."

Sorry had seen a Coast Guard buoy tender tie up to the *Sumner* yesterday.

"Do you speak any English?" the white man asked.

"Some. I'm learning," Sorry said.

"Then we'll talk in your language. I'm John Garrison."

"My name is Sorry. This is my sister, Lokileni. We'll take you to Tara."

Dr. Garrison followed them and the jabbering small children up the beach toward Chief Juda's house. There were so many daily visitors now that adults seldom paid attention to new arrivals. The Dr. Garrison parade, children trailing, reached Juda's in the middle of an argument between Tara, Lieutenant Hastings, and the chief.

"Make him sign a piece of paper saying we can return here in two years, make him do it," Tara said. "They promised."

The lieutenant did not understand a word of Marshallese and was becoming exasperated. Also, he was not accustomed to dealing with a woman. His khaki shirt showed sweat stains.

With Lokileni and Sorry, Dr. Garrison stood a few feet away, listening, head cocked to the side.

Later Sorry learned that Hastings had come to Juda to say that an LST, a landing ship tank, which could carry a lot of cargo, would take a group of their men, building materials, and equipment to Rongerik in a few days to begin work on the replacement village.

Juda said, "It is too late to ask them anything."

"It's never too late," Tara insisted, carrying on for Abram.

Hastings interrupted, "I don't know what you two are talking about, but I'm telling you to pick as many men as you want to help with the construction."

Tara translated.

The Seabees, the navy construction corps, had already designed the new village.

"You have to help make your own homes," he said.

Tara said bluntly in English and then in Marshallese, "We're talking about you signing a piece of paper saying we can return here in two years."

"I'm not signing any paper," Hastings said. "We own this island now. It's a U.S. possession. We took it from the Japanese. You'll do what we say."

Tara stared at the officer, then said calmly, "Suppose we refuse to leave."

Lieutenant Hastings took a deep breath. "Then we'll march everyone onto the LST. You're going to Rongerik, all of you! Believe me!"

Tara translated for Juda and then said, "Oh? At gunpoint, Lieutenant?" She seemed to be enjoying the argument.

Hastings reddened and fought to control his temper.

Dr. Garrison took advantage of the lull and said, "Excuse me, I'm John Garrison. I was told on the *Summer* to contact Tara Malolo." He spoke in Marshallese.

"I'm Tara Malolo."

They shook hands.

Garrison introduced himself to Chief Juda and said, "I'm from the National Museum, part of the Smithsonian. I'll be all over the atoll for the next few months to take samples of bird, sea, and island life, then do 'before and after' studies."

"Why the pistol?" Tara asked. Scientists did not usually carry guns.

Dr. Garrison laughed. "To shoot birds. Made it myself—I have three other barrels for it. I'll try to take at least three specimens of all the wildlife, then come back here in six months, after the bombs go off, and make health comparisons. I just wanted to let you know I was here."

"If you need help, call on me," she said with a smile. "You'll find a lot more birds on Nantil, the next island north."

Garrison thanked Tara for the offer and went out to explore Bikini. He was the first of dozens of scientists who would descend on the atoll. Sorry and Lokileni followed him out, anxious to see him use the odd-looking pistol.

As they left, Sorry heard Tara say to Lieutenant Hastings, "You haven't answered my question about the guns."

The two atomic weapons for the aerial shot and the underwater detonation had been assembled at the Los Alamos laboratory, the same lab that had produced the Trinity test bomb and the ones used in Japan. The new bombs awaited a ship ride to Kwajalein.

Crossroads was appropriately named: Science had opened the door to the atomic age, and mankind was at the crossing of roads that might lead to peaceful use of the atom or to death and destruction around the globe.

8

A day later, at twilight, Sorry and Lokileni sat in the sand where the council building had been and listened to Tara relay the day's news. "The military station in Kwajalein isn't saying very much about it, but Honolulu is. Protests are starting." She had dialed in NBC–Honolulu on shortwave after the Armed Forces Network broadcast.

"People are writing to the president and to the navy, senators, and congressmen. Some newspapers are saying not to drop the bomb. Some atomic scientists say to cancel the tests; they'll prove nothing. The destruction and death they'll cause is already known. There's a lot of talk about us, about Bikini."

"Are you telling us the tests might be canceled?" Sorry's mother asked.

"I'm only telling you what the radio said," Tara answered. "But if enough people protest, maybe the navy will postpone the tests or call them off. There is still a chance."

"That's wishful thinking," said Leje Ijjirik sharply.

"It does no good for the people to raise their hopes, Tara," said Chief Juda.

"And how do we know that she is telling the truth?" Leje asked.

"Come and listen for yourself," Tara replied evenly, calmly. Leje couldn't understand a word of English.

The news session ended a few minutes later. Aside from Leje and a few others, almost everyone was still hoping that something miraculous might happen to put off the dreaded hour of departure. Grandfather Jonjen conducted prayer services at sundown, asking God to save them.

———

On February 25 a landing ship tank 327 feet long, veteran of the Marshall Islands' battles, crunched up on the beach. The bow doors swung open and the loading ramp was lowered. Sorry had never seen a ship like the LST 1108, an ugly, bulky thing.

It was the day the villagers finally surrendered, accepted their fate, acknowledged the power of the navy and the giant government it represented. They'd been foolish to think things could be otherwise, as Leje had said.

The 1108 carried enough food to last a month on Rongerik. Thirty thousand gallons of fresh water. Tools, lumber, cement, tent frames; wooden floors for twenty-six dwellings. There were corrugated sheets of iron for water catchments and many other things that they'd never seen. The navy had taken charge, down to the last nail and bag of cement. The villagers were bewildered.

Sorry willingly helped carry the new pandanus thatch that had been woven by the women. The dismantled pieces of the church and town council buildings went into the lower tank deck, along with the matting. Lokileni and Sorry worked side by side, saying little.

In late afternoon, the 1108 pulled up her loading ramp and closed the bow doors. Her smoky diesels began spinning the two propellers, and she backed down off the sand. Twenty-two men had volunteered to go to Rongerik for a week, to help the Seabees construct the new village. The men stood on the bow, near the forward gun tubs, waving good-bye, their faces solemn.

All others stood on the beach to see the 1108 depart. They watched until the shape of the tank ship began to dissolve in the distance.

Sorry momentarily wished he were going along. He didn't know about anyone else, but he had mixed feelings during these last days on Bikini. He was overwhelmed with the Americans and all their possessions. He couldn't judge them as harshly as Abram had done. What he was wishing was that he were on the 1108 and that they were going not to Rongerik, but rather to America.

————

After touring Dr. Garrison around the island, showing him the cemetery and Abram's fresh grave with its new headstone, the Japanese barracks, and the bunker where the soldiers had killed themselves—after walking him from one end of the island to the other—Sorry and Lokileni became his helpers. Into the canvas knapsacks went starfish and sea urchins and sea cucumbers and shrimp and crab, examples of every living organism they could find along the lagoon shore and over on the barrier reef.

"Why?" Sorry asked.

"Well, we want to know how the radioactivity from the bomb will affect living things on the atoll. If we know what happens to the fish, crustaceans, birds, plants, and coral, then science can perhaps answer some questions about the future of living with atomic weapons."

"I'm not sure I understand," Sorry said.

Dr. Garrison thought a moment. "Radiation, of course, is invisible. You can't see it, hear it, or smell it. But once it gets inside your body you can become very sick and even die. It all depends on how big a dose you get. You ever heard of leukemia?"

Sorry shook his head.

"It's a blood disease. White blood cells can multiply uncontrollably in certain conditions. It's one of the most dreaded forms of cancer, particularly among children. But no age is immune. Leukemia can sometimes result from prolonged deep X-ray treatments and other unusual exposures, like atomic explosions."

Sorry still didn't really understand. White blood cells? He didn't know they existed. "Will that happen to us?"

"No, because you won't be here, but the fish and plants and trees, even the sand, could become sick. There's something called fallout, tiny airborne pieces of radioactive debris from the explosions. The tiny pieces can get into the seaweed of the lagoon. A fish nibbles them and can become sick if it nibbles enough. The fish may glow. You eat the fish, you become sick."

Now Sorry knew clearly why Abram had been so worried. Eat poisoned fish? He said sadly, "I wish America wouldn't drop the bombs here."

Dr. Garrison looked around at the peaceful lagoon, the quivering palm fronds, the beauty of the island. "One part of me agrees with you. But the scientific part doesn't. I'm anxious to know what will happen to the fish, the plants, the trees . . ."

———

One afternoon Sorry stopped Dr. Garrison for a moment at water's edge.

"Tara said you know a lot about the atom bomb."

"Actually, I know very little," said Dr. Garrison.

"Do you know how far away any humans were when they tested that first bomb?"

"Six miles, I've heard."

"Was anyone killed or hurt by it?" Sorry asked.

Dr. Garrison shook his head. "I don't think so."

"They'll drop the bomb here on a lot of ships?"

"Yes, but on one in particular, a battleship, the USS *Nevada*."

"The plane will be high up?"

"About five miles, I've heard."

"How will they see the battleship?"

"They have very powerful bombsights. They'll see it, Sorry. I'm glad you're so interested."

From that plane trip to Rongerik, Sorry knew it was easy to see things from the air. He'd seen the schools of tuna. The men in the bomber would be able to see him down on the lagoon.

"Thank you," said Sorry. "I'll be here in the morning."

"Thanks again for all your help," the scientist said, smiling.

In Pearl Harbor, the USS *Nevada*, bombed and beached during the Japanese attack, was being painted a bright orange-red, with white stripes around the main deck edges. After the December 7 attack, she was repaired and refitted, and fought in World War II. Now the thirty-five-year-old battleship would be zeropoint, in the center of the target fleet. The aerial bomb would explode above her single stack.

9

Sorry sailed Dr. Garrison over to Nantil Island in early morning, and the scientist shot seven different types of birds with that strange-looking gun by noon. The *Sumner*'s cooks fixed him boxed lunches each day, and he always ordered extra boxes for Sorry and Lokileni. But she'd stayed home that morning for school.

Over lunch Dr. Garrison said, "Since we can't test humans out here, we'll use animals."

He said that in several months a special troop transport loaded with animals, a navy Noah's Ark, would arrive. They'd take the place of humans.

The navy was always doing strange things, Sorry thought.

"Pigs will be used because they are comparable to us in hair and skin. Goats will be used because their body fluids are similar to those of humans."

"They'll be killed?" Sorry asked.

"Those on open decks will be killed instantly by the explosion. Others will just be radiated and then studied later by doctors. Others inside the compartments may not be harmed at all."

The troop transport would serve as the animals' home until they were transferred to twenty-two of the target ships a few days before the bomb drop, Dr.

Garrison said. They would replace sailors in usual battle positions throughout the ships. "White rats will be in engine rooms and living quarters. The National Cancer Institute is providing some special white mice that are prone to cancer and others that have seemed to resist it. After the aerial shot, they'll be flown back to Washington for study and breeding. Some might not be able to breed again."

"Because of that poison you can't see or hear or taste?"

He nodded. "Radiation."

"Can't they do it any other way except by killing animals?"

"Unfortunately, no. But I'm really fascinated by what they'll do. They'll dress some of the pigs in gunners' antiflash suits and smear them with regular antiflash solutions. Some of the goats will be shaved and daubed with creams. A goat blood bank is being collected to treat the radiation victims."

"Will the animals be loose on the ships?"

"No, Sorry. The rats and mice and guinea pigs will be in wire-mesh cages. Over six thousand are being built. The pigs and goats will have pens. The navy is buying five thousand bales of hay."

Sorry had never heard of guinea pigs or some of the other animals. There were no white mice on Bikini. But the thought of animals being radiated shocked him.

"Things far beyond our imaginations are going to happen here," Dr. Garrison said. "Big planes, bomber types, will fly through the radioactive cloud without pilots. They'll travel from Eniwetok and return, without any human aboard."

"How will they do that?"

"Radio remote control." He paused. "War is a terrible thing, Sorry, but it causes all kinds of advancements in science, medicine, weapons, communication, aircraft, even food. And something called television, pictures moving by electronic transmission, has been perfected in the last ten years. We'll use it for the tests."

"Not a movie?" He and Lokileni had seen their first movie on the afterdeck of the *Sumner*.

"Yes, but different. I've read it'll be coming into homes in five or six years."

"Will we see it here in the atolls?"

"Not for a long, long time, I'd guess."

Disturbed, Sorry said, "Why has the world left us so far behind?"

"Because of where you live. But in some ways you've been lucky. And a lot of people think they'd like to live on an island like this one. Few could do it. They'd starve."

"Will we ever catch up?" Sorry asked, frowning.

"I hope not. But if you do, I hope you'll do it slowly. There've been times when I wished the airplane wasn't possible, and I wished the atom bomb hadn't been invented, and maybe sometime I'll even wish that television didn't exist."

He was beginning to sound like Grandfather Jonjen. "How can you make those wishes? You're a scientist . . ."

"The things I usually study aren't modern. Most date back a million years, in one way or another."

It was time to bag more birds.

———

After returning to Bikini Island, Sorry sat beside Dr. Garrison near the canoe house, again waiting for the landing craft to take the scientist back to the *Sumner*.

139

Sorry asked where the bomb would be dropped.

"So far as I know, about three or four miles straight out there," he said, pointing to the lagoon. "That's where the *Nevada* will be, according to what I've heard on the ship."

"Yesterday the radio said there'd be between ninety and a hundred other target ships."

"That's what they told me in Pearl Harbor at the briefing. They're bringing some big ones in. Even captured Japanese and German ships. A couple of aircraft carriers, *Independence* and *Saratoga*. A bunch of submarines and destroyers. All kinds of ships."

"Just to blow them up?"

"Test them," said Dr. Garrison. "See if they can get hit by an atom bomb and still fight. No one knows what will happen, Sorry. That's the spooky thing."

Sorry nodded gravely.

"They don't want anyone killed out here. Hiroshima and Nagasaki scared everyone, even the scientists who made the damn bombs."

"They should be scared," Sorry agreed, thinking, *I am.*

"They plan to explode it five hundred feet above the *Nevada* when a B-29 Superfortress drops it."

Then the landing ferry pulled up on shore, and Dr. Garrison returned to the *Sumner*.

Thousands of letters were sent to U.S. President Harry S. Truman and members of Congress. Even though Bikini was five thousand miles from California, people were frightened by Operation Crossroads. Would the bomb blow a hole in the earth's crust and allow the ocean to pour in, stopping the planet's rotation? Would all the seas turn bright yellow from radiation? Would the bomb burn up the oxygen in the atmosphere? Would there be a tidal wave in Hawaii? The navy hoped to win over public opinion through use of radio and newspapers.

10

A few days later, a navy newsreel team filmed the final village Sunday church service. The newsreels would play in movie theaters around the world, making audiences believe that the people of Bikini approved of the tests.

The villagers always dressed up on Sundays. The girls and women wore leis. Tara had on a Hawaiian print, and Lokileni wore her only white dress. Sorry's mother wore her best dress, white with tiny purple flowers on it. Sorry had on his only white shirt and white pants. Most of the girls and women had red hibiscus in their hair. They looked pretty but were not smiling.

Hymns were sung, and Grandfather Jonjen read from his Bible and preached while the cameras whirred away. The service was held not too far from where the church building had been, and Jonjen led everyone in prayer from his crude bench and table—the altar—asking God to spare the island and keep the people safe on Rongerik.

The service did not go well, since the newsreel crew kept moving the camera around, asking Tara to have Jonjen move this way or that way, look this way or that way, say again what he'd just said. Grandfather Jonjen was confused and Sorry was angry.

Finally, Tara rebelled. "That's enough!" she shouted in English.

Sorry felt the hours and minutes ticking away. Their time was almost up, every moment now was precious. The 1108 would soon push back up to the beach.

Several photojournalists had arrived from New York, and Tara interpreted for them. At the same time, she tried to tell the islanders' story, how the navy had deceived them.

"But the reporters don't listen," she told the villagers. "They seem caught up in what the navy is going to do. They wanted to know if I thought the bomb was going to blow all our palm trees down. I said that dried fronds might blow off but the trees would just bend. They all kept asking stupid questions like that—even typhoons don't blow palms down. None of them are really interested in us losing our island."

The writers stayed for a few days, then a flying boat returned them to Kwajalein.

Tara said that almost every newspaper in the world would have stories about the atom-bomb tests; about the simple, trusting people of the tiny village, isolated for decades from civilization, suddenly swept into modern times. The international airwaves were filled with radio broadcasts in every language. Thousands of still pictures were taken, in addition to black-and-white newsreel footage.

———

On the morning of March 6, the villagers gathered again in their best clothes, swept the cemetery clean with fronds, and picked the last flowers that were blooming to decorate the graves. Grandfather Jonjen held a service to honor the dead, especially Abram Makaoliej, and bid them farewell for a while. Still cameras flashed and motion picture cameras rolled. Grandfather Jonjen, in the midst of honoring the dead, was asked to move toward a large white gravestone. Sorry saw Tara close her eyes in rage.

Then a *Sumner* landing craft brought Commodore Wyatt and several other officers ashore, plus Azakel, the governor's interpreter. Azakel went straight to Chief Juda, ignoring Tara. He told Juda that the governor would like to reenact the scene of February 10, the day that the villagers agreed to give up their homeland to please the Lord, for the newsreel cameras.

Juda agreed as Tara walked away, furious.

Sorry thought about following her but didn't. He wanted to see what else was going to happen.

Azakel told everyone to go back to where they'd been that Sunday three weeks ago. They went, like the sheep Abram had described. Wyatt sat on a palm bole, old Lokwiar sat on a box; everyone else sat in the sand. Leje Ijjirik was wearing his Japanese soldier's hat.

The scene of that fateful February day was reenacted several times, to be used for navy public relations purposes.

Sorry heard Azakel tell everyone to smile. He noticed that only a few people did. Most sat looking down at the sand. Were they ashamed at being chased off their own land? Or were they just numb? Sorry didn't know.

Before the cameras were put away that day, they were focused on children playing in the lagoon, laughing and shouting, having great fun. Lenses were aimed at any smiling faces that could be found. Anyone seeing the films of those faces would think the villagers were quite content to give up Bikini so that all mankind could learn more about the atom bomb.

Watching the filming, Sorry thought that Abram would have shouted, *"Letao!"* Liars.

So he did.

The Fifty-third Naval Construction Battalion, a thousand men, the famed Seabees of World War II, builders of everything from barracks to entire air bases, had orders to arrive in early March. They would change Bikini to an atomic test site with their bulldozers and welding torches and electric saws and concrete mixers. To help in such work, twenty dump trucks and three cranes were to be put ashore. They would look odd on the scenic village main street, rolling over the crushed pink coral.

‖

Maybe it was just his imagination, how his mind was working that morning, but the dawn of March 7, 1946, was one of the most beautiful Sorry had ever seen. Jonjen awakened them, and Sorry and Lokileni, joined by Tara and Mother Rinamu, Jonjen and Grandmother Yolo, went out to the beach to watch the sun come up. There were folds of low clouds to the east, and the sun turned their curled, dark toppings to yellow-gold as it rose. The sky, a deep, deep blue, seemed to touch the ridges of gold. A warm breeze was blowing, feathering the lagoon with small whitecaps.

Then the other villagers came out of what was left of their dwellings, now just stark frameworks with a few old sun-bleached thatch roofs left, to join in a final, silent viewing. They stayed on the beach until the sun was well above the horizon.

After all that he'd said, so many times, about wanting to leave the atoll to see the *ailiñkan*, now Sorry desperately wanted to stay.

———

In the late morning they began to load all their possessions into the 1108. An amphibious vehicle called a

Duck made trips from what used to be their houses into the ship, small children riding on top of the loads, having the time of their lives. They were shouting and laughing. The laughter of the children was the only laughter that afternoon.

Sorry and Jonjen very carefully carried the chest of drawers and placed it in a safe spot on the lower cargo deck. Also the fine wooden chair from Nantil. Most of their other things were bundled into matting.

More unplaited pandanus was carried aboard by the armful, and more sheets of corrugated iron from the Bikini cisterns were hauled by the Duck.

Except for the small children, everyone was busy, and the American newsreel cameras rolled once again. Back and forth the villagers went to the 1108, until everything had been stripped.

The outrigger canoes were the last to be loaded. The huge crane lifted them up like they were feathers and lowered them gently to the main deck. Sorry helped secure them.

When Lokileni was a little girl, Mother Rinamu had made her a rag doll. Lokileni had named her doll Leilang. As she and Sorry took a last look around the place where their dwelling had been, she said to Sorry, "I've been thinking about Leilang and where to leave her."

"Why leave her?" Sorry asked.

"I want something of myself to stay here. Maybe she can watch over our land until we return. But where to put her?"

Sorry felt a lump in his throat. "How about wrapping her in *sennit* and putting her up high in that palm?" He didn't know what else to say.

"Do you think the wind from the bomb blast will blow her out?"

He looked at the soiled old doll, then at his sister's troubled face. He sighed and said, "How about putting her in the ravine? Then the hot wind will just sweep across her."

Lokileni sighed, too, and shook her head. She put the doll against her cheek and fought back tears. "No," she said, and tried to smile, then knelt down.

He watched as she kissed Leilang good-bye and sat her in the sand, her back against a dwelling upright. Lokileni looked up, eyes glistening.

Then it was time, close to two o'clock, to board the 1108. But as they walked toward it as a family, they realized that Grandmother Yolo wasn't nearby.

They'd seen her less than a half hour ago while they took the last armloads to the main deck. They searched the beach and called her name. She had a habit of wandering off.

The few people still onshore joined them in looking for her.

Jonjen suggested, frowning, "Her favorite rock?" It was on the ocean side, of course, the rock on which she sat to communicate with the spirits of the sea.

Sorry joined his mother, Tara Malolo, and Lokileni in scrambling in and out of the ravine. A worried Jonjen stayed behind.

Soon they could see the rock. Her frail figure wasn't on it: the ocean beach was deserted. The rumbling rollers were high this day, topped with white fringes; they crashed on the reefs, throwing up spray that sparkled against the sky.

They searched along the reef for almost an hour, but there was no sign of Grandmother Yolo. She was not hiding. She had joined Sorry's father in the ocean grave and would never have to face Libokra.

Weeping softly, they held each other in sorrow.

Then, slowly, they went back to the lagoon to tell Grandfather Jonjen. Trembling, he looked in the direction of the barrier reef, closed his eyes, said a silent prayer. Finally, he said, "I should have gone with her."

———

Dr. Garrison had come in from the *Sumner* to wish them good-bye. He'd brought simple gifts from the ship's store for Tara, Lokileni, and Sorry.

Sorry's mother and Jonjen went aboard the 1108, heads bowed.

Sorry and Tara talked for a few minutes with Dr. Garrison. Then Tara said, "Please tell us the truth. When do you think we can come back here?"

Dr. Garrison looked slowly around the island, then finally back at Tara. "No one knows. Maybe never," he said with sadness.

Maybe never! The words cut into them, draining them. The truth, at last. They could feel the enormity of what he'd just said. *Maybe never.*

They managed to say farewell to Dr. Garrison and shook hands with him. Then, as they walked toward the LST, Tara said to Sorry, "Tell no one. There must be hope."

The tank ramp was drawn in, the bow doors were closed, and the diesels began rumbling at the stern. Acrid smoke blew across the boat as the engines were started. They were sailing with the tide.

Dr. Garrison stood within a cluster of officers and enlisted men on the sands. They were waving good-bye. Then he turned his back and began to walk toward what was left of the village, appearing unable to watch the scene.

Soon the 1108 began to pull back, going in a half circle as the water deepened. Most of the villagers were lining the port rail on the top deck. Sorry looked around through a glaze of tears and saw that even the older men were fighting emotion. The hurt gripped chests and throats. Hands were held to lips.

It was Grandfather Jonjen, mourning the death of Yolo, who began to sing. The others joined him.

> *O God, our help in ages past*
> *Our hope for years to come*
> *Our shelter from the stormy blast*
> *And our eternal home.*

Tara reached over and took Sorry's hand. He put his arm around Lokileni's shoulder, and his jaw quivered as the voices faded back into silence.

Tara stared at the island. Her eyes blazed with anger.

As they passed it, the starboard rail of the *Sumner* was lined with officers and sailors waving good-bye. Some of them turned away, too.

The outbound course was near where the *Nevada* would be anchored.

They went past Bokantuak and Eomalan and Rojkora, where Abram and Sorry had met the giant tiger shark; then on past Eonjebi and out into Enyu Channel.

As the noisy diesels pounded away and the islanders watched, Bikini became smaller and smaller and smaller and smaller, until it finally disappeared.

The 1108 rocked on through the night, sounds of the sea slapping against her steel sides. Bodies on matting were scattered over the main deck, each family staying close to their possessions.

Tara chose to remain on the foredeck, lost in her thoughts, staring into the darkness. Sorry went up there in early evening and stood by her. After a while, Sorry's mother came up to stand beside Tara, and Sorry went below.

Soon he was side by side with Lokileni on the cold steel of the main deck, which was made for tanks of war, not sleeping people. They lay stiffly and silently on their mats, feeling the chill dew, missing the softness of sand.

There was now an airstrip on Enyu, carved out by bulldozers. Other ships of the support fleet were also arriving; at least two thousand sailors went ashore every day for recreation in what was once Bikini village. The village had almost vanished. Five concrete basketball courts had been poured. There were four baseball fields and ten volleyball courts where palms once fluttered in the wind. There was an officer's club and an enlisted men's club serving ten-cent beer. "Radio Bikini" was broadcasting daily to the world from the island. Bikini had been totally Americanized.

12

In the morning, not long after breakfast, with a school of porpoise romping around the bow, they sighted a small island just outside Rongerik lagoon: Bok, guardian island of the atoll. Sorry knew the voyage would soon be over. They'd passed Tara's home, on Rongelap, during the night. At least now she'd be just eighteen miles from her family.

The foredeck was soon jammed as the passengers eagerly looked at the main island before the anchor was dropped. The beach was wider than Bikini's, and one area was covered with red hibiscus—always a good sign. The palms and pandanus trees didn't look too bad from the distance. With the sun shining brightly, they could see the white tent roofs of the dwellings, their new homes. The church and community buildings, including Tara's school, had been erected. From a mile away, it looked like a good island.

Tara came up behind them. "We can't go to the beach until the tide is higher."

So they spent the day impatiently, sitting, walking around the ship, talking, looking toward shore. Sorry was anxious to see where they'd live.

"If the wooden floor in the new dwelling bothers you we can always take it up and sleep on the sand," his mother said.

Sorry said, "This lagoon bothers me. You could put it between Rojkora and Enyu, and not have room for a canoe race." He was sounding like Abram.

"It is much smaller," she agreed, "but let's hope it'll be full of fish."

"I haven't seen many so far," he said, and walked away in disgust.

Chief Juda, Manoj Ijjirik, and Tara rode a landing craft to the beach to mark each family's dwelling. Before they left, Tara said, "Not everyone is going to be happy with where we locate them." The idea was to keep the families in more or less the same groupings they'd had on Bikini.

Sorry's mother said, "We can always trade."

———

The tide became high about five o'clock, and the 1108 got under way for shore, the big nose shoving up on the beach a few minutes later. After they found the tent house with "Sorry Rinamu" marked over the doorway in red crayon, they began to carry everything to it. Thick brush was still around the housing, though a lot had been cleared away by the Seabees.

The sailors rigged floodlights, and laden with goods, the people moved between the LST and their dwellings. Salt mist coated everything.

The next morning, Lokileni helped around the house, unpacking what little they had, while Sorry worked with the few remaining Seabees to build several more cisterns.

In the afternoon, they went off to explore the new island. After they'd walked a ways along the lagoon shore, Sorry said worriedly, "Where are the fish, Lokileni? Where are they?" He had his father's eye for locating them.

They didn't see the great schools of small fish that were always chased by larger fish in the Bikini lagoon. They walked close to the waterline and didn't even see very many *jebak*, the useless lizardfish that usually prowled the bottom near shore. Nor could they see any halfbeaks feeding on algae.

Sorry said, "Maybe they're just not around this island."

There were other islands, of course. But it was disturbing to see a tropical lagoon where so few fish were evident. More than that, it was frightening.

They walked into what looked like the thickest of the palm groves. There was a lot of brush around the palms since they hadn't been tended in years. Tara had said the people of Rongelap came over to pick coconuts but didn't stay to work in the groves.

Sorry and Lokileni went back out to the beach and slowly circled the entire island in less than an hour. Near the village they heard children screaming and began running toward them. A Kejibuki boy of maybe four was on his back at water's edge, holding his right foot up in the air. His arms thrashed and he rocked on the sand. All of the children were crying, but he was wailing the loudest. Flapping on the sand in front of him was a stonefish, the most poisonous kind of all. A spine had entered the child's foot while he was wading.

Sorry scooped him up and ran to the navy medic who was with the half dozen Seabees still on the island. The wound was cleaned and the boy was given a tetanus shot, but by nightfall he was near death.

Slowly, the boy recovered, but Sorry soon discovered that other poisonous creatures swam in the lagoon—the beautiful zebrafish, *kale*, and the ugly scorpionfish were plentiful in certain areas.

———

Everything bad that they'd heard about the atoll now seemed to be true. The palms were older, and many weren't productive. The coconuts were smaller, and there weren't enough of them to make copra production worthwhile. Even the coconut husk fibers weren't strong enough to make good *sennit*. The pandanus trees didn't have as many leaves. There were no taro pits. Maybe Grandmother Yolo was right. Perhaps the *ekejab*, the evil Libokra, did still lurk in the lagoon with the stonefish and hover over the lagoon at night.

By the end of the first week, they were already unhappy and homesick, but Chief Juda kept insisting that things would soon be better.

The houses had a paint odor and their floors creaked. The navy canvas locked smells in. Sorry complained, and his mother said, "Let's take the tenting down." The usual thatch walls would go up instead.

"We have to leave here. We have to go back home," Sorry said.

"That's impossible."

"I'm not so sure," Sorry said.

His mother looked at him and frowned.

About 5,000 white rats, 204 goats, 200 white mice, 200 pigs, and 60 guinea pigs were to be placed on certain target ships three days before the bomb drop.

13

Lieutenant Hastings had given Tara a navy safety pamphlet on radioactivity that had been prepared for the Crossroads press corps. She'd gone over it a half dozen times, trying to understand it. Finally she brought it to school to use as lesson material for older students.

Sorry listened through a window.

" 'There are two types of radioactivity. One is natural, the other man-made. With natural radioactivity, we are bombarded every day by rays from the sky. And, in some areas, natural radioactivity comes from metals like uranium ore.' What will happen at our atoll is man-made . . ."

She saw that the class was lost already and put her hand to her forehead.

"All right, an atom bomb is a bomb whose explosive force comes from a chain reaction based on nuclear fission, this time using a substance called plutonium, made by man. It's very complicated . . . and . . . I'm sorry . . ." Shaking her head, she folded the pamphlet and said, "I tried."

Frowning, upset with herself for not being able to explain in simple terms what the scientists had written, she added, "The world would be a better place if they hadn't discovered how to make such a terrible weapon."

Then she shifted to English lessons.

Sorry's mind wasn't on the lessons. He kept thinking back to what Dr. Garrison had said about the disease called leukemia, and how the fish and plants and trees could become sick.

————

What enraged Tara the most was what the navy was now saying to the world. She had a new American-made radio set and generator, given to them by the commodore. She listened each afternoon, scribbling away.

At one evening news gathering—the same as they had held on Bikini—she said bitterly, "An admiral in Washington told reporters today that we're adjusting nicely over here. Said we're completely happy. He said Rongerik is a bigger, better island than Bikini. *He's never been here!*"

As the long days were passed in trying to adjust—and the villagers did try very hard—the navy flew newspapermen and radio commentators in from Bikini to cover the "primitive natives," as one reporter said.

"We are natives, all right, but not from the Stone Age," Tara said.

Every time correspondents arrived, Tara would try again to tell them exactly what had happened on that Sunday in February.

"They have Hawaiian disease," she said to Sorry. "All they see are the palm trees and the lagoon. They hear guitar music that isn't here. They look around and say, 'Not a bad place to live,' and fly back to Bikini with their portable typewriters and suntan oil."

In mid-June, Sorry began to paint Abram's stolen outrigger and sail. The villagers could understand the new coat for the canoe but wondered why the sail was being painted. It would be stiff and difficult to handle, everyone knew.

When asked, Sorry just smiled widely and said, "To brighten up the sea."

No sailor of the Marshalls would ever be satisfied with that answer. No sailor would ever do anything to cut the speed or handling of a canoe.

"You're up to something," Manoj Ijjirik said, observing the brush spreading the red lead over the mainsail.

"You'll know soon, Manoj," Sorry replied.

He'd thought of little except the bomb drop over the last few weeks. He'd gone over it and over it in his mind—when to sail, how far away to be when the bomber flew over. He was confident they'd see him down there, a splash of vivid red against the blue sea. The newsmen would tell the world about it instantly; the navy would postpone the test. Then the navy would find another place for the tests and everyone could go back to Bikini. There'd be no radiation poison falling on it. It would work, Sorry was convinced, and it was all Abram's idea!

Tara came down to the beach. "You were serious, weren't you?"

Sorry was on his knees, wielding the brush. He straightened up. "Yes, I was very serious."

"Does your mother know? Does your grandfather know? Does Chief Juda know?"

Sorry shook his head. "I'll tell them when I tell everyone else."

"This is insane, Sorry. Abram probably wouldn't have tried it, after all. It was just something he dreamed up out of frustration."

"I don't think so. I think he believed it would work."

"You have more intelligence than that. The navy isn't going to call off the test because of a single red canoe in the lagoon. All those ships! All those men! It's costing millions . . ."

"We'll win by simply getting in the way, like Abram said. They won't drop the bomb. The newspapers and radio will report it, and they'll find another place."

Tara sighed and shook her head in dismay. "I thought you had more sense than to even think more about it. Abram would be the first to say don't do it, Sorry. Do not do it . . . ."

"My mind is made up. I'll sail two or three days before the test, then hide out on Lomlik. During the night, I'll sail closer to the target fleet. I can put the canoe within six miles of the *Nevada* and still be safe."

"Who said that?"

"Dr. Garrison."

"Did he know why you wanted that information?"

"No," Sorry admitted.

"You should talk about this in the council."

"It won't do any good."

Tara started to walk away, then turned and frowned. "Are you certain that Dr. Garrison said you could come within six miles of the *Nevada* and still be safe?"

"That's how far people were away from the first bomb test."

She shook her head. "This is ridiculous."

She watched him painting for a moment longer, then returned to the canoe and sat down on the rail. "What makes you think they'll see you?"

"Dr. Garrison said they have powerful bombsights. And I'm going to polish one of the Japanese tins so they can see flashes when the sun shines on it."

"Oh, Sorry . . ." Worry and frustration spread over her face.

"Tara, my father would have done it. He was not a coward. Neither am I."

On a cloudy June 24, *Dave's Dream*, the B-29 Superfortress that would carry the Able bomb, made practice runs over the target fleet. *Dave's Dream* dropped a harmless practice bomb and hit the *Nevada* almost bull's-eye. The Able bomb was similar to Fat Man, the one dropped on Nagasaki. It was eleven feet long and weighed over 10,000 pounds. Painted on the casing of the bomb, which would soon unleash tons of deadly radium over the quiet lagoon, was the name Gilda, a Hollywood movie character played by the beautiful actress Rita Hayworth.

14

Grandfather Jonjen blew his conch shell to again gather everyone for Tara's nightly news report.

"They'll now drop the bomb July first at eight-thirty," Tara announced.

The shot had been postponed twice for unknown reasons. This time, Armed Forces Radio said all the target ships were in place with animals on board, and the bomb was waiting on Kwajalein, guarded by marines.

Sorry's pulse quickened.

"How big is that bomb?" Manoj Ijjirik asked.

"I have no idea," Tara replied. "The radio said it will be the same size and type as the one they dropped on Nagasaki. They called that one Fat Man."

Fat Man. Sorry got a mind picture of a huge-bellied bomb spewing up an atomic cloud.

———

By now, late June, they were in the wet season, always a blessed time in the northern Marshalls. Rain pelted down on the new roof of the church.

The white men had all gone back to their support ships for the blast. Before departing, Lieutenant

Hastings promised that no one would be in any danger on Rongerik. An LST would be waiting in the lagoon to take them to safety if the cloud laden with particles of plutonium came that way.

Other questions were asked, and Tara tried to answer them as best she could, looking at her broadcast notes.

Would they hear the bomb go off? She didn't know.

Would they see the flash? She didn't know.

Would the cloud look like any other cloud? She didn't know.

Would rain fall from it? She didn't know.

The villagers were asking impossible questions. Few of them had ever used a phone or lived with electricity or ridden in an automobile, and they were desperately trying to understand what the white men had suddenly brought into their lives.

After the news report, Sorry stood up and took a deep breath. Then he said in a steady voice, "I'm going back to Bikini on Friday. I'll be on Lomlik Sunday night. I hope to be within six miles of the *Nevada* on Monday morning. I hope they'll see me and call off the bomb—save our island, find some other place."

For a moment, there was dead silence. The villagers could not believe what they'd just heard.

Mother Rinamu, quickly getting to her feet, said, "You'll do no such thing, Sorry. Have you lost your mind?"

Leje Ijjirik laughed hollowly. "Even if they see you, they'll drop the bomb. One crazy boy in a red outrigger. That won't stop them."

Chief Juda said, "That sounds like something Abram would do. You got the paint from him, didn't you?"

"Yes, and the idea," Sorry quietly admitted.

"We might have known," Leje said with disgust.

Tara stood up and said, "I'm going with him. Abram was right. We have to protest what's happening out here."

Sorry was astonished. Tara was coming along?

Leje said, "Two crazy people . . ."

Everyone was now looking at Tara. She moved to stand by Sorry.

Then Grandfather Jonjen hoisted himself up on his crooked stick. "I'm going, too," he said.

Manoj Ijjirik rose up and asked for volunteers to man a larger canoe.

No hands came up. No voices spoke.

So much for Sorry's idea of having the whole village sail to Bikini. He looked around at the 160-odd faces before him. There were frowns and more looks of disbelief: looks that said, *You're crazy, Sorry Rinamu!*

Tara broke the trance. "We're simply thumbing our noses at the giant." She put her thumb up to her nose, wiggled her fingers, and drew needed laughter.

The people lingered after the announcement and talked to Sorry and his mother and Tara and Jonjen. They wanted to be part of what was going to happen at their atoll, yet none had changed their minds about going.

Even Manoj Ijjirik didn't volunteer to ride in the red canoe.

"Why are you coming?" Sorry asked Tara later, still surprised at her decision.

"I think someone has to protest, as Abram said. I

couldn't let you do it alone. And I now think it will work. I really think it will."

Then Sorry asked Jonjen why he was coming.

"Someone has to be there to pray."

———

The next morning, almost everyone went down to the beach to look at the canoe, unable to believe where it was going to go, what it was going to do.

Sorry answered the same question—"Are you sure they'll see you?"—again and again. His answer was yes.

At noon, Tara went to the community house, where the new radio was kept, and started the generator so she could listen to the news and recharge the battery. Sorry and Lokileni went with her.

Soon she said, "They're moving everyone on Wotho and Eniwetok to Kwajalein, just in case the wind blows the wrong way." The weather report indicated clouds and rain over the northern Marshalls for Friday, Saturday, and Sunday. The villagers were expecting their "safety" LST to show up by Sunday night.

Sorry said, "I think we can sneak right into the lagoon without being caught."

He'd use the regular white sail to make the voyage from Rongerik to Bikini, then change to the red one at Lomlik.

The target ships lay quietly at anchor about four miles off the Bikini beach. The *Nevada* was at zeropoint position, and not far away were other battleships—*Pennsylvania, New York,* and *Arkansas*—in their standard navy gray. The carriers *Saratoga* and *Independence,* veterans of wild air battles, were there. Foreign ships included the ugly Japanese battleship *Nagato,* squatting like a huge toad, and the sleek German cruiser *Prinz Eugen,* probably the finest warship afloat. Others were spread out from zeropoint roughly in a wagon-wheel formation.

15

The more most of the villagers thought about it and talked about it over the next four days, the more the return to Bikini seemed so heroic, so daring, that it could not fail. It was a way of telling the whole world about a small band of people who were helpless against a giant.

There they were on a spirit-ridden little island, feeling abandoned by the Americans, feeling the Americans had stolen their land, and believing that they were certain to starve in not many months. Rongerik could not support them, they knew. And this was a chance, perhaps their only chance, to say, *World, look at us. Look at what you've done to us!*

Sorry heard the talk and felt encouraged by it. Mother Rinamu was now thinking that way, talking that way, proudly reminding everyone that it was her son who was going to stop the bomb. Even Leje Ijjirik became quiet.

———

Sorry walked along the beach with Lokileni the morning of June 28, not long after sunrise. Beneath all his hero talk were doubts and fears.

"Are you certain you want to go?" she asked.

Without the slightest hesitation he answered, "I'm certain, Lokileni."

"I'm frightened for you," she said. "If you get too close . . ."

"I won't. *Jimman* will tell me when I'm six miles away."

He hugged her, and then she went off to join the women and children picking red hibiscus in that one area of Rongerik beach—the only nice part of the island, some thought. A path of flowers would be made from the church down to the outrigger.

The canoe was ready, with chunks of baked tuna and grated coconut and bottles of fresh water, plus a dozen K-ration boxes—combat rations—left by the navy. There were mats to sit on and sleep on. They were taking fishing gear to catch meals along the way. The voyage shouldn't take more than seventy-two hours, if the wind was favorable.

Sorry spent a few minutes with his mother, embracing her, telling her not to worry, that he would see her in about six days. She smiled at him through brave tears and said, "Take care of yourself."

Then the villagers went to a church service. Grandfather Jonjen read from the Bible and prayed for God to protect His children and allow them to change the minds of the white men and convince them not to drop their terrible weapon over the home lagoon.

Then they sang "Amazing Grace," faces toward heaven.

After the service, Sorry led Tara and Jonjen, each wearing leis and warrior headbands, down the hibiscus path to the canoe. That was in the tradition of the old

171

tribes, who went off to war in fifty-foot canoes, with their clamshell axes.

The villagers lined up on either side of the path, clapping hands and wishing them well. Even Leje Ijjirik was there slapping his palms together.

Sorry's confident face seemed to be wreathed in gold from the early sun, the way the leaders must have looked when sailing two hundred years ago—strong and handsome.

Good-byes were said, the lateen sail was raised, and the canoe, with Jonjen and Tara in it, was shoved out into the water by many men. Sorry leapt in.

He broke out in a wide smile and held his fingers up in the sign that the Americans had taught them, the victory sign. The villagers kept waving until the red canoe with the white sail grew dim on the horizon and went out through Bok Pass.

On June 30, a reminder signal went out from the command ship, *Mt. McKinley*, "One July Is Able Day." Within minutes, final preparations were made on instrumentation ashore and aboard the target ships. The pigs, goats, caged rats, mice, and other animals were in their assigned positions. In the late afternoon most of the support ships still in the lagoon began to leave. A few stayed behind to check on the target vessels and make certain all personnel had been taken off. The support ships were assigned to areas east and northwest and would stay in those relative positions until after the bomb drop. The *Mt. McKinley* had been code-named *Sadeyes* and the silver-colored bomber, *Dave's Dream*, had been code-named *Skylight One*.

16

The clouds hid the red canoe on the way to Lomlik. Now and then they'd hear the sounds of aircraft engines above; there seemed to be dozens. One sounded as if it would break through the low clouds. At times, there was light rain.

Looking up at the cloud cover, Tara asked, "What are they doing?"

Sorry had no idea.

If the clouds parted and that aircraft found them, they'd likely be reported, be forced to turn back. The radio had said that all sea traffic had to stay at least 150 miles away from Bikini during the next three days.

Sorry stayed to the north of the atoll and sighted Nam, then Worik; and finally, at sundown Sunday, there was long, skinny Lomlik, where the Rinamus owned land. The clouds had pulled back in midafternoon, and by twilight the canoe was in the home atoll.

Bikini Island was only a smudge, but even in the poor light of sundown they saw that the face of the lagoon had changed completely. In the far distance were the anchored dark forms of the larger ships, the aircraft carriers and battleships.

Most of the "live" ships had departed, leaving the

"dead" ones, many with animals aboard, to wait the night out. A tower with a big instrument on top was mounted on Lomlik, facing the target ships. Sorry had an eerie feeling as they pulled near its steel legs. It looked mean and hateful in the shallow light.

Sorry had been to Lomlik dozens of times to pick coconuts, Jonjen many more times than that. Jonjen looked around their land. He said, "The white men always seem to spoil whatever they touch."

They were home—but they weren't home, because this wasn't home to them anymore, wasn't the lagoon that Sorry had grown up in. It was a foreign water now under a foreign flag. They couldn't see any change on Bikini itself; it was too far away in this graying dusk. But they knew the change was there. The beautiful lagoon had turned hostile, its outriggers replaced by warships.

They talked very little. There was not much to say. What could be said of the bomb, and of the bomber that would be up there tomorrow morning with a Fat Man in its belly?

They ate K-rations, and just before bedding down, Sorry said, "Have you changed your minds? If you have, go over on the barrier beach in the morning. If I can't stop the bomb, you'll be safe there, I think."

Tara said, "We're going out with you, Sorry."

Jonjen said, "I didn't come all this way to sit on the barrier beach."

"I want to head for the target fleet not long after midnight," Sorry said.

They stretched out on their mats, and soon Grandfather Jonjen, at peace with his world, was snoring away, as usual, under the stars.

Neither Sorry nor Tara could sleep.

Sorry said, "When I was seven, we knew the typhoon was coming. The old men, like Jonjen, could tell it was coming our way by the looks of the sky and by how the breeze was blowing, the smell of the air. The birds vanished from the atoll and even the fish went to the bottom. I'd heard about typhoons from Jonjen and was so frightened I could hardly speak. After a time of total silence, with not a whisper of breeze, it roared in, sending us up the palms and destroying the village. I feel like that now, Tara. Frightened, suddenly. It's so quiet here; the lagoon is so black."

She said, after a silence, "I was thinking yesterday that we were too young to die. Why should we take this chance? About halfway here I thought about asking you to turn back. Then I thought about what Abram would do. He would keep going, I knew, and he would shake his fist at the navy."

"That's what I thought, too, when that plane came so low. Abram would keep going. So we've come all this way and must go out there tomorrow morning and hope they'll see us . . ."

Sorry finally dozed off.

Around two o'clock, he awakened Tara and Jonjen to say, "Let's put the red sail on."

That took about ten minutes.

Then they ate K-rations again and were ready to go, Tara and Grandfather Jonjen climbing into the canoe.

Sorry shoved off and caught the light breeze, sailing south toward the target area in the pitch-dark lagoon.

They didn't speak, worried that the white man's electronic ears might hear them. Ears that Dr. Garrison had described.

Book III
The Bomb

At 5:43 A.M., July 1, on Kwajalein, the four engines of *Dave's Dream* mumbled sweetly as it taxied out to the long runway, the atom bomb tucked in its belly. Then the engines began to roar as pilot Woodrow Swancutt opened the throttles. *Dave's Dream* quivered at runway's end while all the instruments and dials were checked one last time. Finally, the brakes were released and she began to roll, gaining speed until liftoff.

At dawn, under high scattered clouds, they hid in their canoe by the stern of a ghostly LST that was anchored about three miles off the beach, north of the *Nevada.* Sorry had often fished in almost the exact spot.

As the sun slowly began to light up the abandoned island, they could see the south end no longer bore any resemblance to what they'd once called home. Even from three miles away, the high steel towers and buildings were plainly visible. The navy had only left a few palms here and there.

It didn't seem possible there could be such change in five months.

Grandfather Jonjen glared at the island as if the devil himself had made the changes.

Tara turned and finally whispered, "Do you realize we are the only humans within miles of here?"

———

It was a few minutes after eight o'clock on Tara's watch when the sky suddenly filled with all sorts of aircraft. Bombers, seaplanes, fighters. Sorry had no idea what they were doing. Some were at low altitude, so the three of them sat in the canoe, hunched down, hoping they wouldn't be seen yet.

"They'll land a seaplane and jerk us out of here," Sorry whispered.

His idea was to raise the red sail close to when the bomb was scheduled to drop, and steer north, away from the *Nevada*. He worried about the breeze.

Tara asked, "Will we be six miles away?"

Sorry nodded. "I hope so."

Grandfather Jonjen said he'd estimate the distance to the huge target ship, glowing in its red coat, and wait until the bomber could be seen before beginning his prayers.

"Please be certain," Sorry said. Six miles was critical.

Then the other planes went away, and the three of them faintly heard a sound from above. They looked up to see sun flashing off a silver bomber.

Sorry said, "I think that's it."

Dave's Dream *arrived over the lagoon at 8:26. "This is* Skylight One, Skylight One. *Ten minutes before first simulated bomb release. Stand by. Mark: Ten minutes before simulated bomb release. First practice run."*

Sorry and Tara ran up the red sail and the wind caught it. They shoved away from the LST, and Sorry steered north, watching the sky, saying, "Remember, the radio said they'll make several practice runs. Maybe they'll see us down here."

To Grandfather Jonjen, he said, "Tell me when you think I'm six miles away from the *Nevada*."

The wind wasn't helping.

"This is Skylight One, Skylight One. *Five minutes before actual bomb release. Mark: Five minutes before actual bomb release . . ."*

Sorry said to Tara, "Start flashing the tin lid. They'll see it."

Eight-thirty had come and gone.

Waiting, Sorry thought about the unknowing animals, the goats and pigs that were shaved and smeared with antiflash ointment; about the white mice and white blood cells and leukemia; and about the fish that might glow. . . .

"Skylight One. Skylight One. *Two minutes before actual bomb release. Mark: Two minutes before actual bomb release. Adjust all goggles. Adjust all goggles.*"

Tara stared at flashes of sun reflecting off the bomber in the blue sky. "Look down, please look down here, please look down here . . ."

On the battleship USS Pennsylvania, *a metronome was inches from an open microphone, counting the seconds, heard around the world.* Tock, tock, tock, tock, tock . . .

At that precise moment, Sorry realized the madness of what they were doing, the madness of where they were, the madness of trusting Jonjen to put them in a safe position.

Up there in the aircraft, the pilots would be looking only at the USS *Nevada.*

Nothing around it!

Not a single tiny red canoe moving slowly north.

Madness!

They were insane. The three of them in their crazy war canoe were insane.

Grandfather Jonjen, eyes closed, was holding his Bible and praying. Sorry and Tara stood and looked up at the flashes and prayed. God alone could save them now.

"Skylight One, Skylight One. *Coming up on actual bomb release. Stand by! Stand by! . . . Bomb away! Bomb away. Bomb away . . .*"

The light from a million suns flashed over the lagoon, then there was a clap of thunder so loud that it burst eardrums.

A second later, Sorry, Tara, and Jonjen seemed to be encased in shining glass, wearing skins of glass.

From the center of the target ships rose a ball of violent red, turning pink, streaked with chalk white. It grew rapidly, like an evil flower, a huge, whitish pink rose with a white stem lengthening by the seconds, becoming a giant ice-cream cone.

Becoming a white cauliflower.

Becoming white death.

The animals didn't even have time to scream.

In a moment, the heat wave, a wind from hell, caught the red sail and thrust the canoe across the water as if it were a balsa chip, blowing the sail out as if it were a loose kite.

A moment later, a ten-foot wave hurtled across the water, tossing the outrigger up, then throwing it down angrily.

The wave traveled with a wet hissing sound.

Then there was total silence in Bikini lagoon.

———

The Able bomb had spent its energy, had spewed its poison.

Its killing had only begun.

A Factual Epilogue

The explosion took place within a few millionths of a second. Soon, drone planes with Geiger counters began flying over the atoll, listening for the inevitable radiation clicks; then drone boats, also equipped with counters, wound among the target ships. Some had been sunk; others were heavily damaged; some were burning; but most were still afloat. Several hours later, slowly, carefully, support ships edged back into the lagoon, the men aboard listening for the Geiger chirps.

About 10 percent of the animals were killed instantly. Others would die, in time, from radiation. Still others would never bear offspring. Soon, aboard the Noah's Ark ship, there would be a poignant scene: a shaved radiated goat would be strapped to a table for a blood transfusion.

———

By mid-July of the next year, the food supply on Rongerik was so low that the villagers were cutting down palms to eat the hearts. What fishing there was couldn't feed them.

A gruel made from coconut meat, coconut water, and flour mixed with cistern water was the primary diet by

February 1948. The navy flew in emergency food. The villagers were then moved to Kwajalein and spent the next seven months there while Chief Juda and the other *alab*s searched for another home.

Finally, they decided to go to Kili, 450 miles away. A "wet" island, Kili has fine palms, breadfruit trees, and even bananas, but no lagoon or harbor. It is completely surrounded by barrier reefs, and on many days even small boats cannot land. Many of the world's first nuclear nomads still live there, almost fifty years after the Able shot. Isolated there, more than six hundred descendants of the displaced Bikinians face a dark future.

In 1969, President Lyndon B. Johnson announced that Bikini Atoll was "safe" again for human habitation, that the United States no longer had any interest in it. A group soon left Kili and upon arrival in the lagoon was shocked to see the condition of the islands. One *alab*, tears in his eyes, said to a government civilian, "What have you done to us?"

The palms were mostly gone. There were skeletons of abandoned, roofless buildings, breezes blowing through open windows. There was junk and scrap all over what remained of the atoll. Broken concrete, oil drums, rusting trucks, cranes, and steel towers. The Defense Department had turned the islands into waste dumps.

A small number of the original families, including a few Rinamu men, were determined to resurrect Bikini from the nuclear dead. They cleared the waste and began life again. They stayed on the main island for almost ten years, until doctors discovered they were being poisoned by Cesium 137, a radioactive material in the sand. Another awful mistake had been made by

194

government agencies in Washington, D.C. As of April 1995, scuba divers explore the target fleet wrecks on the bottom of the lagoon, but the island itself is still poisoned.

The adult children and grandchildren of the relocated Bikinians are still to be found in the Marshalls, mostly on Kili, but on other islands as well; in Hawaii and California; and some in Nevada.

A few of the older people still dream of the Bikini they knew as children. They have a word for it—*lamoren.* Ancestral land.

Author's Note

On Writing
THE BOMB
By Theodore Taylor

The Bomb has waited for paper and ink for almost half a century, twisting and turning in my mind since the months after atomic bombs were dropped on Hiroshima and Nagasaki. In late 1945 the U.S. Navy began searching for a suitable place to explode the world's fourth and fifth nuclear bombs. The site chosen was Bikini Atoll, in the Marshall Islands of the western Pacific, twenty-two hundred miles from Hawaii.

Operation Crossroads sounded interesting. Almost one hundred unmanned warships would gather in the atoll's lagoon for two "shots"—one aerial, one undersea. Navy officials wanted to know if the ships would survive the cataclysmic force of nuclear explosions. Animals would take the place of human crews on the target ships. Goats would be tethered on the open decks; guinea pigs and five thousand rats would be inside the ships, along with the cancer-prone white mice. Some of the goats and pigs would be shaved and smeared with antiflash compounds. (Goats and pigs have skin similar to humans'.) All would be exposed to radiation.

In early February 1946 I boarded the USS *Sumner*, an ancient submarine tender that had been converted for geodetic survey work. She had printing presses aboard for making navigational charts. A combat veteran of the Pacific war, she'd run with the invasion fleets. For Crossroads our crew would rechart Bikini lagoon, erect navigational towers, plant buoys, and destroy the coral heads that rose from the sea bottom, which could be hazardous to the incoming target vessels. The *Sumner* was the first Crossroads ship to arrive.

The atoll waters were a bright cobalt blue, and the sands of the main island, Bikini, were a stunning white. Palm trees fluttered in the warm wind. I remember the stillness and peace, the incredible beauty. Outriggers glided around the lagoon. Fish jumped. Seabirds winged by.

I remember thinking: *Are we really going to drop an atomic bomb on this beautiful place?*

There were four drag teams, each operating a forty-foot boat, seeking out those dangerous coral heads, locating them so divers could place dynamite charges to blow them up. I commanded one of those teams.

On February 10, 1946, an amphibious aircraft landed near the *Sumner* carrying the military governor of the Marshall Islands—a navy commodore, one rank below rear admiral. He went ashore to inform the 160-odd natives that the navy needed their atoll for testing two atomic bombs. Knowing they were a religious people, the commodore invoked God to persuade the islanders to go *temporarily* to another atoll. God would approve of such a move; it would help mankind understand atomic power. Most of the people meekly agreed. After all, the navy had freed them from Japanese occupation. White men had ships and guns and aircraft; the Bikinians grew coconuts and speared fish. They could return home in several years, it was said. They were lied to, willfully or not.

A few days later I went ashore and circled the entire island of Bikini, from the lagoon shore to the ocean barrier reef. I visited the village, with its thatch-roofed houses. The people were still friendly and smiling, though they were losing their homeland in what would become a modern Trail of Tears. I felt ill as I took a landing craft back to the *Sumner*.

On March 7, less than a month after the commodore first visited, a landing ship tank (LST) backed away from the beach carrying the entire population of Bikini Atoll and all of their worldly possessions. For hundreds of years their people had slept on pandanus mats on the sand, and their possessions were indeed few.

As the LST passed near the *Sumner*, the people were singing a hymn, looking back at their island. They were bound for Rongerik, an uninhabited atoll 120 miles away. I remember their voices, their fears. There wasn't a dry eye on our ship, and most of us were hardened combat veterans.

More than a half-century later the surviving displaced islanders and all of their children and grandchildren are still nuclear nomads. Their homeland is still poisoned by radioactive fallout; cesium 137 lies deep in the sands.

The Bomb is loosely based on what occurred at Bikini Atoll. I found the book terribly difficult to write.

Theodore Taylor
Laguna Beach, California

Reader Chat Page

1. Although he's thousands of miles away, Sorry Rinamu is intrigued by the *ailiñkan* and their modern way of life. What fascinates him about Western culture?

2. Sorry is worried about taking his father's place on the tribal council. What makes him change his mind?

3. Chief Juda is reluctant to question the U.S. military's intentions, let alone to resist in any way. Why is he so willing to follow along with their demands?

4. Why does it seem that Uncle Abram is more capable of understanding the potential of the U.S. government to withhold information from the Bikinians?

5. Why do you think the Bikinians agree to be relocated? Do you think they had any choice in the matter?

6. Sorry becomes worried about the future of Bikini Atoll when he sees two warning signs: a moaning albatross and Grandmother Yolo's ominous message from the *tournefortia* tree. What do you consider to be "warning signs" in your culture? Are you ever superstitious?

7. Do you think the Americans had the right to choose the Bikini Atoll as their testing site?

8. What does it signify when Lokileni leaves her doll on the island?

9. Why does Sorry's teacher, Tara, decide to accompany Sorry and his grandfather in the red canoe?

10. If you were in Sorry's place, would you have done what he did?